Troubled Waters Ahead

<u>Troubled Waters Ahead</u>

By: Derek Miller

Copyright © 2015 by Derek Miller

All rights reserved. No part of this book may be reproduced by any process whatsoever without written permission of the author/copyright owner.

This book is a work of fiction. Names, characters, places, and incidents either are products of the author's imagination or are used fictitiously. Any resemblance to actual events or locales or persons, living or dead, is entirely coincidental.

Ten years ago, Gary Moyer became only the third person to successfully navigate the 40 mile Gunnison Canyon section of the Moose River. He had a special talent and everybody knew it, including a young aspiring adventurist friend, Blake Henson, and an up and coming photo journalist/TV producer Nathan Garner. What would motivate people to go on a suicide adventure trip through unimaginable river conditions making a documentary of a river adventure? Is it the possibility that media types want a lot of glory and adrenaline rushes; with little skill, ability and preparation for extreme risk? Where does good common sense, logic, ethics and the desire to be famous come into play? Is it possible to have all of the above and still survive in a hostile environment? What was to be a once in a lifetime adventure trip down one of North America's wildest rivers turned into a trip of desperate measures and wilderness survival.

Dedication

To my wife Kathleen, son Derek, and daughter Brittany, with love.

"We're commercial river guides. We take people down the river; we make it possible for those people to do the things that they would never dream of doing in their life."

"We take people to the edge, and we hold onto them as they look over, and then we pull them back again."

- Gary Moyer

<u>The River Wild</u>

The River's calm,
as it's flowing straight.
Beyond the bend,
awaits your fate.

Debris is scattered,
among the riverbed.
Through the crevasses,
is where the water's fed.

Listen carefully,
for the rapids sound.
Around the curves;
is where they will be found.

The water's deep,
the current's strong.
If you hit a boulder,
everything could go wrong.

Boaters must maneuver wisely,
there's no time for hesitation.
They must use their knowledge and instinct;
if they want to reach their destination.

Thank you to my wife Kathleen for writing this poem which I feel captures the true essence of river travel.

Table of Contents

Preface

1. The Legend
2. Mentor Meets Protégé
3. Big Sky Regatta
4. Wheels in Motion
5. Ausable River Canoe Marathon
6. Opportunity Arises
7. Reigniting the Passion
8. A Team Again
9. Adventure and Its Side Effects
10. Another Variable to the Equation
11. The Yukon 1000
12. A Feat to Be Proud Of
13. The Need for More
14. Three's A Crowd
15. The Mighty Moose River
16. The Run of Their Lives

17. High Drama on the Moose

18. Survival Mode

19. Search and Rescue

20. Perseverance

21. Salvation

22. Conclusion

Glossary

Preface

I don't know how many times I would mumble to myself the words; "uh oh, trouble up ahead". It is especially common for me to utter these words when I'm racing in my kayak or leisurely paddling my canoe downstream on a river. I have always had a strong fascination of rivers and the unique characteristics and features that each and every river presents. I've learned from paddling in hundreds of rivers that not only are they all different but each one demands respect and various specific skill sets to properly navigate them. My passion for rivers has always been fueled by the fact that they change day by day. They are dynamic and constantly evolving.

Rivers are perhaps Mother Nature's best example or source of revealing her wide range of attitude and personality. The fact that one minute you may be experiencing such calm, peaceful water, and then in no time you are caught in the most furious water you've ever been in, has always compelled me.

I've been in and around rivers all my life so it was a natural progression for me to write a story on the interactions of rivers and the people who play or work on them.

Rivers are complicated enough but when you throw the human element into the mix it becomes even more intriguing. People constantly push the envelope when it comes to adventure and knowing what their limitations are. Who, what and when determines enough is enough.

The balancing act of common sense, logic and morality has been a struggle for human kind ever since Adam and Eve. This story features these struggles through three main characters; Gary, Blake and Nathan.

The interaction of the characters highlights their desire for respect from their peers, notoriety and their never ending obsession to raise the bar. Questions are raised throughout the story that will cause you to wonder if it is possible for these characters to be on the same page with each other. For instance, is it possible that Gary, Blake and Nathan have the same motives, objectives, skill, desires and respect for each other?

The story will expose the characters selfishness, ego, greed and other common human shortcomings. You will see the impact that their actions will have on friends and loved ones.

I thank my wife Kathleen for being the love of my life and my rock of stability. Thank you for inspiring me and motivating me to write this book.

You have worn many hats in this whole process; to include editor, proofreader, poet and cheerleader – Thank you so much. I love you.

A special thank you goes out to my daughter Brittany, for taking on the role of copyeditor.

1

The Legend

"Look out! Didn't you see that log?" exclaimed Gary. "You have to let me know whenever there's a log floating in the river like that. We could have tipped over on that one. Heck, I'm in the back and I could see the darn thing". Gary continued on his rant, making it clear that part of being in the bow* of the canoe is to pay attention to all obstacles in or out of the water. "You have even the slightest indication that something is out of the ordinary; you need to let me know", he continued. Blake, who has been the target of Gary's rants, has only been out paddling two or three times in his entire life. Gary on the other hand, has been paddling for over 30 years. He has paddled in just about everything from rowboats, rafts, canoes, kayaks, dories, drift boats, duckies; you name it, he's paddled in it. After all, one of his passions in life was being outside and being on or in the water enjoying nature to its fullest.

Gary had said many times before that he never saw or paddled a river he didn't like. Regardless of what is going on in his head, once he hears the sound of a river; he stops to pay full attention to the sight, smell, sound, taste, and feel of the river. There is something about the sound of a river that harnessed him in and held him hostage. He would say that the sound is hypnotic and that it is so therapeutic. Hearing water; swoosh on, over, and around pebbles, rocks, boulders, and trees captivated him. No matter what river he was on, or around, he always felt a sudden surge of "man it's great to be alive". Sometimes he would find himself purposefully seeking out rivers for no particular reason.

Gary Moyer was a legendary figure in the tight-knit fraternity of canyon boatmen, largely because of an adventure he embarked on in late May of 2004; when he defied logic, common sense, and the Canadian National Park Service; by successfully navigating The Gunnison Canyon section of the

Moose River; in the Northern Yukon Territory. Gary was well acquainted with the Moose River long before his legendary run, as he was a river guide on the Moose during the months of May through July; when he was on summer break from Montana State University. He loved it so much that after his four seasons of guiding during his college years; he continued on for three more seasons.

Gary is a 39 year old plumber from Bozeman, Montana. He has always had a passion for the outdoors; especially kayaking/canoeing the many splendid and scenic rivers of Montana. Gary felt that he was kind of a lost soul, a man without a country, a loner, etc. He always had a hard time saying where he was from. He never lived in one place for more than a few years. As a child, he and his mother moved from town to town quite often; never really establishing any roots in one particular area. By the time he reached 27 years old he decided to permanently settle down in the Bozeman area. Even his name sake was a mystery. He never knew his biological father and his step father was a person he would just as soon not talk about. However, he found the bureaucracy in changing his last name was a mountain of paperwork; so he just kept the name the same, even though he had no connection whatsoever to it. Gary is a fierce competitor and has little patience or tolerance for mediocrity. Needless to say, he has been competing in sporting events all his life.

Gary is married to Jennifer who is a nurse practitioner at a local hospital. Gary and Jennifer have been married for 8 years and have two children; Courtney who is 4 years old, and Peyton who is 6. Jennifer also loves the outdoors, but never really gets a chance to enjoy it due to her busy work schedule, children, and volunteer work.

Early on in the marriage both Gary and Jennifer were quite active in participating in local canoe races and road racing events. In fact they would often enter canoe races that offered a mixed class division so that they could compete as a team. If the race didn't have a mixed class category they would compete in the C-1 solo canoe class or K-1 solo kayak class. Over time their commitment to raising a family, work, friends etc. made it difficult for them to compete together.

Jennifer was finding it increasingly hard to deal with Gary and his authoritative personality. Between Gary's intense competitive nature and Jennifer's happy go lucky style, they mixed like oil and water. After a race in Spokane, Washington, Gary threw a tirade in front of fellow competitors over Jennifer's lack of intensity. He lashed out to her that she didn't seem to take the race serious enough and perhaps she really wasn't interested in winning at all.

In another episode, in a race on the Madison River near Three Forks, Montana, Gary had become irate over Jennifer's paddling technique. "Quit bobbing your head so much, you're rocking the bow* and causing turbulence. Keep your head still and limit your movement up there." "Shut up, I'm tired of listening to your complaining", Jennifer yelled back to Gary. "If you don't like my paddling up front, why don't you paddle up here and I'll paddle in the stern".

When it comes to paddling, Gary is a bit of a control freak and usually insisted on being in the stern* position while Jennifer was always in the front or bow position. This way, he can maneuver the canoe more efficiently and also to ensure that both their paddling strokes were in sync. The more they paddled together, the more they clashed. The only time they paddled together was when they brought the kids along to spend time together as a family on a lake near their home.

It got to the point where Gary seemed to go out of his way to keep Jennifer on the outside looking in when it came to his many outdoor activities and paddling events.

The friction that was going on between the two of them didn't just present itself in the canoe, it was alive and well in the home as well. They simply did not see eye to eye and never really seemed to be on the same page. Jennifer was more than happy to excuse herself from paddling with Gary all together and in-fact, she even helped in finding her replacement.

2

Mentor meets Protégé

She already had somebody in mind that she thought would be a compatible match for Gary. Jennifer volunteered to set up a little get together at their house so that they could meet each other and to discuss the possibility of paddling together. Gary being moderately open to the idea; asked Jennifer who it was. She said, Blake Henson, a physical therapist who has known and worked with Jennifer at the same hospital for the past six years. Much like Gary, he is an avid outdoorsman and adventurist who loves to compete. Gary had actually met Blake a few times during several hospital Christmas parties, summer picnics and other hospital functions.

During the get together Jennifer could tell that Gary and Blake hit it off well and appeared to be on the same wave length. In fact she even overheard them talking about getting the canoe out on the river to do some training. Blake had emphasized to Gary that he had virtually no experience canoeing with the exception of a few times when he was a boy scout. Gary did not seem to be concerned and suggested to Blake that he would be a pro in no time. Even before getting out in the canoe with Blake for the first time, Gary had big plans. His sights are firmly planted on a 60 mile canoe race in eastern Montana that is to take place on Memorial Day. The race will require a great deal of skill, fitness, determination, perseverance, communication and good chemistry between the two paddlers. Something Blake and Gary don't have much of at this point. However, they still have a good amount of time before the big race.

The last of the winter snow had recently melted away giving them their first real window of opportunity to get out and get a feel of each other's strengths and weaknesses. For Blake there are many weaknesses to be exploited as he has spent very little time in a canoe. As mentioned before he had only ventured out a couple of times as a boy scout.

At first they paddled on a nearby lake to practice turning and basic stroke techniques. For Blake it was a bit awkward but eventually felt a comfort level finding his own stability and rhythm. Of course they were practicing on a calm wide open flat water lake. The real test will be when they have to navigate through tight narrow turns, strainers*, low hanging branches and various other obstacles of the river. Gary felt confident that Blake had the stamina and fitness to complete a single day 60 mile race, but could he read the river; could he be technically sound and paddle efficiently? He knew that extensive time on the river together and practicing strong communication skills was going to be critical.

"Look out! Didn't you see that log?" exclaimed Gary. "You have to let me know whenever there's a log floating in the river like that. We could have tipped over on that one. Heck I'm in the back and I can see the darn thing". Blake was quick to say that he was sorry and that he would be much more alert from now on. Another learning lesson for Blake occurred when he instinctively grabbed hold of a low hanging tree limb to avoid getting hit from it. Within seconds both Gary and Blake were in the water – prompting Gary to lecture Blake on why you should never grab anything above or anything to the side – especially low hanging branches/limbs.

Blake was hoping that he wasn't too premature in deciding to commit to Gary and to compete in this race. There was a bit of uneasiness for Blake not really knowing all the dynamics of working with Gary and dealing with his ultra competitive and controlling personality. Although he had been given prior warning from Jennifer that Gary can be a touch of a control freak, he had dealt with much worse at work and past acquaintances. Gary was going to be a choirboy compared to the authoritarian surgeons he worked with on a daily basis.

After several more training runs on the river and a few eight mile runs the two sat down to work out all the details for the 60 mile race. Jennifer already volunteered herself and Chelsea Snyder a friend of hers from work. They would act as the team's pit crew and would provide encouragement and support throughout the race. The pit crew would be responsible for supplying Gary and Blake all food and liquids as well as extra paddles, bailers*, sliding seats, first aid needs, etc.

Gary felt that this upcoming 60 miler would be a great initial objective for Blake as the river was relatively flat, slow and had very few rapids. It was definitely going to be a great introduction into the world of marathon canoeing. If anything was going to bond the two of them it was going to be a 60 mile canoe race that would take at least eight hours or more to complete.

  Over a 60 mile race many factors come into play for determining the end result. Besides the obvious factors such as experience, physical conditioning, skill, weather, pit crews and equipment; the condition of the river will be the primary factor in determining overall race times. Conditions such as overhanging branches or fallen tree limbs will create bottlenecks, causing many delays and potential portages. Backwater, sucking or swirling water, shallow water, and excessive river debris will hamper any momentum and will slow down the best of paddlers. More importantly, the higher the volume of water in the river the faster the race times will be; a lower volume of water in the river will result in slower race times. All of this is what Gary hammered home to Blake to confirm how dynamic a river can be.

3

Big Sky Regatta

After four hours of driving in a Chevrolet Suburban loaded with two Jensen Kevlar racing canoes, eight carbon fiber paddles, seven life preservers, and coolers loaded with food and drinks they had arrived at the starting area where they were to campout for the night.

After setting up their camping arrangements Gary and Blake decided to get a feel of the river and to practice for the first portage which was about five miles downstream. At the first rapid they came to, there was a group of paddlers that had pulled out onto a gravel bar below them. From the back Gary stuck his paddle in the water and began steering the canoe into the current while Blake, up in the bow, began pulling the front around. Wham! To be followed by a few curse words was all you heard – a rock had caught them both by surprise. In disbelief, they felt the boat hesitate for an instant, balanced on a boulder like a see-saw on a fulcrum. Then, with a whoosh, the upstream side of the canoe dipped under, the canoe filled with water, and into the chilly river they went. Both Gary and Blake thrashed around like a King Salmon caught onto a fishing line. After a few moments of thrashing around they eventually found their footing. Fortunately, the water was less than a couple of feet deep. This was not the start that neither Gary nor Blake envisioned, luckily for them it was only a trial run. At first Gary was disgusted with the whole ordeal but seeing that they were unhurt and the canoe appeared to be okay, he just shook his head and said "let's make sure this doesn't happen tomorrow".

After returning back to camp and getting into warm clothes Gary suggested to Blake that they had violated the second rule of canoeing through rocks:

when the canoe gets hung up and turns sideways, always lean over the downstream gunwale (side railing of the canoe), not the upstream gunwale. Gary added that the first rule was, "avoid the rocks"! It just goes to show you that no matter how long you have been paddling it only takes one split second of a lapse in judgment and just like that – you're in the water.

Although the practice run was a train wreck their spirits all in all were positive and upbeat. They spent the rest of the afternoon working on the canoe and their drinking system. Dinner consisted of a heaping pile of spaghetti to get their necessary carbohydrate levels built up. Blake and Chelsea spent a great deal of time at dinner communicating in an intense manner prompting Gary to reiterate to everybody that this was not a double date and reminded everyone that there was a big race ahead of us. Before going to bed Gary and Blake went over last minute details of the race and to make clear what specific duties Jennifer and Chelsea would perform as the teams pit crew.

Gary could tell Blake was a little on edge and tried to put Blake at ease by suggesting that the main objective was to finish the race and to finish in one piece. Blake agreed but expressed to Gary that he didn't want to let him down. Needless to say

Blake did not sleep well that night and was excited to get the race over with.

At 7:00 AM the gun fired, officially starting the Big Sky Regatta. For the most part the race was somewhat anticlimactic, even the problematic first rapid from the day before went smoothly. Even the three portages went fairly well with the exception of the final portage. While carrying the canoe over their heads Blake tripped over a moss covered rock causing Blake to fall hard. The bow of the canoe went down with Blake leaving him with a sprained ankle, lacerated knee and some front end damage to the canoe. Fortunately they were able to patch up a small cut just below the water line on the right front. Gary and Blake were thankful that Blake's injuries were not severe enough to prevent them from finishing the race. Even more critical was the fact that they had no more portages to contend with, meaning that Blake would not have to get out of the canoe to walk or run until after the race was completed. Even the three pit stops went off without a hitch. Don't be confused with the term "pit stop". During the so called "pit stop", Gary and Blake paddle forward while Jennifer and Chelsea move along with them at the same time handing over drinks – usually Gatorade and food items such as bananas, protein bars, trail mix etc. Essentially Gary and Blake do not stop at all, if anything they slow their stroke tempo down just enough to receive the supplies and quickly resume to their racing pace.

Their overall finishing time was eight hours twenty-six minutes. Not too bad considering the incident at the third portage and Blake's limited experience in a canoe not to mention racing in a marathon. They finished in 15th place out of 28 canoes in their class. Nevertheless, Gary looked at the event as a success and was pleased with Blake mastering the learning curve that every new paddler has to face. Most important, Gary felt that their communication and chemistry were terrific.

Chelsea was intrigued with people having the desire to paddle 60 miles, and couldn't resist asking Blake his impression of the race. Blake responded that over the course of 60 miles he experienced the full spectrum of feelings and emotions that a person could ever imagine. The pre-race jitters/nerves, fear, the adrenaline rush at the sound of the start gun, frustration at not getting off the lake (where the race started) in a good time. The pain – anguish, muscle spasms from mile 20 on, dehydration and cramping from mile 30, headaches and mental fatigue from mile 40 on, and numbness in limbs from mile 50 on. Blake added that his mind had played various tricks or games to perhaps compensate with his pain and fatigue. But all of his emotions and feelings became moot when they had crossed the finish line as pure joy and elation took over.

4

Wheels in Motion

After receiving their finisher's plaque, patch and BBQ chicken dinner it was time to travel back home to continue on with the daily grind. Needless to say it was a great experience for everybody, and it didn't take long for Gary to propose yet another race that he thought would be a great challenge for them. Jennifer who was driving and Chelsea sitting in the passenger seat started laughing – suggesting that maybe they should take a break and enjoy this. But Gary wanted more, a lot more. This time Gary proposed that they should consider entering the Au Sable River Canoe Marathon. This is an annual 120 mile canoe race that starts in Grayling, Michigan and finishes near the shores of Lake Huron in Oscoda, Michigan. The marathon takes place on the last full weekend in July. The race would require over 16 hours and more than 50,000 paddle strokes and racing overnight. This would be a far cry from the Big Sky Regatta which was exactly half the distance and half the amount of paddle strokes. In addition, there would be six portages as opposed to three that the regatta required. Blake was flabbergasted and suggested that Gary was either kidding or just simply insane. Ever since Gary was a kid paddling in Cub Scout races he had known about the Au Sable River Canoe Marathon and wanted to race in it. Perhaps this race appealed to Gary because of its uniqueness. This race has a lot of components that other races do not have. It is perhaps the oldest canoe race marathon in the United States (first ran in 1947), and is the longest, non-stop canoe-only race in North America. The marathon starts in the dark at 9:00 PM in Grayling in a Le Mans – style start where the competitors carry their canoes in a foot race four blocks through town to the Au Sable River entry point.

    Canoeists come from all over the world. Most racers are from Michigan. The other major areas are

Quebec, Minnesota, Wisconsin, and New England. The race is also considered the world's toughest spectator race as many of the spectators follow the racers overnight down the full 120 miles to the finish.

Paddlers would have to navigate the narrow, winding upper stretch in total darkness, as well as stump – filled ponds and the blazing July sun in the lower stretch. It was obvious to both Gary and Blake that this race was not going to be a recreational canoe float, but a professional ultra – competitive race with the very best professional paddlers from around North and Central America. Gary and Blake will need to be in peak condition in order to complete the race in the allotted time, and to endure the grueling and strenuous physical and mental strains the marathon will demand of them. This was all too much for Blake to comprehend and he refused to commit to Gary. Gary understood, but was nevertheless more than anxious to send in the race registration form regardless. After all the race was less than two months away and Gary knew that they would need at least 150-200 miles or 20 or more hours of paddling a week for training. Gary had urged Jennifer to persuade Blake while at work to enter the race. Jennifer was to have nothing of it and insisted that this was his fight, not hers.

In the meantime Blake and Chelsea had become boyfriend and girlfriend and were together every possible waking hour. They even spent time up at the lake paddling in Chelsea's canoe. Chelsea thought it was ironic that Jennifer was instrumental in getting herself into paddling sports and now it was Jennifer's husband getting Blake into the sport. Chelsea would go on to say that in the past she and Jennifer would participate together in various local races. "All things happen for a reason" Chelsea said to Blake. For some reason all of this was supposed to happen.

Chelsea thought that this upcoming race would be a great experience for all concerned. Not only would it be thrilling for the racing participants but for Chelsea and Jennifer as well. Blake was catching on to Chelsea's subtle, yet clear implications and decided that he would jump on board with Gary for the race.

Not only was the training going to have to be amped up for this race but the logistical planning of it as well. Just the trip to Grayling, Michigan alone was going to be about a 23 1/2 hour drive. They would have to stay overnight in motels for at least four nights, two out and two coming back home. They would camp at least four nights while in Michigan. They also had to factor in extra time for pre race sprint trials to determine the order of the canoes at the start. The trials are held on the Wednesday, Thursday and Friday before the race on Saturday in Grayling. The time trials consisted of each team paddling downstream one quarter mile towards the East Branch of the river. Once there, you must complete a counter clockwise turn around a buoy. Then the racers must head back upstream to the starting point and the next team does not start until the team finishing reaches a point close to the start buoy. On average this can range from two minutes and fifteen seconds to five minutes. The overall finish times can take from about five minutes and thirty seconds to thirteen minutes. Once all of the teams have finished the sprint trials; they will be lined up in groups of five; from the fastest to the slowest, on the night of the marathon to make the four-block foot race.

In Gary's research of the race, he found that first-timers rarely finish. So, he knew based on a very small time-frame window of training that any finish will be respectable. After all, it takes paddlers years to get to know the course. To understand what racing through the night involves, learn how to navigate the vast; unmarked backwaters by compass and map at full speed. They use bow lights when they have to, but amazingly many prefer to paddle in the dark, detecting the ripples of objects with honed night vision.

There was no time to secure financial support through sponsors to enter in the professional division. So the only option was to enter the amateur class; and pay everything out of pocket. The amateur class is rarely contested and in 1993 only one of two boats completed the race. The competitiveness of the race is due to the $50,000 in prize money, the long canoe racing tradition in that part of the country, and the 19 hour deadline in which to complete the race.

Perhaps the moon will help Gary and Blake paddle the river at night. That is if there will be a moon out. Perhaps the faint glow of the night sky against the tree-line, making a dark wall on either side will help mark the course of the river. Blake was extremely concerned of what Gary was telling him. It was bad enough that the race is 120 miles long, but paddling at night just seemed ludicrous to him. They both felt that it was a good idea to get to Grayling a few days before the event to scout the race course and to get a feel of the river; especially at night.

A lot of the information that Gary was learning about the race was via phone conversations with an old Moose River guide buddy, Dale Quinn. Gary and Dale guided on the Moose River together for six years. In fact, Dale loved the Moose River region so much; he took up permanent residence along the river near Whitehorse, Yukon Territory. Dale was also a marathoner both in running and in paddling. He had participated in the Au Sable River Marathon in over 10 races and knew the race inside and out. Gary was extremely confident in talking with Dale, knowing that he was getting the most accurate and most reliable information possible.

Gary and Blake knew that time was precious so they worked out just about every day after work. They would paddle every other day with Saturday being their longest training session. Saturday would usually entail paddling upstream against the current for about 25 miles then back downstream for the same distance; giving them a total of 50 miles. The non-paddling days would consist of cross training and running sessions. Even Jennifer and Chelsea would get in on the fun and paddle with the guys. With the potential of at least 10 sites or pit areas, the women knew they were going to be in for a long haul during the race. But unlike the Big Sky Regatta where the pit crews supply the racers while paddling next to them in the river; the Au Sable pit crews are called feeders; and have to remain along the riverbank. Gary and Blake will need to position their canoe as close to the riverbank as possible so that Chelsea and Jennifer can either hand or toss their supplies into the canoe as they pass by.

After going over all the details and logistics for the trip and race, it was time to pack and head out. They arrived in Grayling on Wednesday to scout the river and make preparations for the race. Not long after setting up their campsites they ran into Dale Quinn, whom like many other racers were staying at the same campgrounds. It was great for Gary to see Dale after not seeing each other for over 10 years. After all they had some amazing experiences working together in The Moose River region. After catching up for all the past years, Dale provided more updated information on the race and proposed to Gary that they scout the river with him and his partner Greg Cantor.

On Thursday both teams left from a canoe/kayak outfitter whose boardwalk serves as the starting line for the race. Dale had learned the day before from locals that this was a high water year and that records could be broken. It appeared that the Au Sable River has a constant flow that varies so little that people build their homes on the riverbank with no danger of flooding. The first 15 miles of the river is a shallow twisting river with a gravel bottom that flowed through pine forests dotted with canoe outfitters and river homes. Both teams found some minor chutes in the river to paddle through which saved some time. After the confluence* of the North and South branch which joins the Au Sable, there is more volume, less gradient and abundance of two to three feet of sucking water (stagnant). After approximately 20 miles they pulled their boats out to be transferred farther downstream. Jennifer and Chelsea had followed them down with the Suburban so they loaded the canoes on the Suburban. Dale felt it was imperative to scout the middle part of the course where there are a series of six hydroelectric ponds. The ponds are shallow and are further characterized by sucking water, dead arms, deadheads (a stump or log that is mostly or fully submerged), and weed-beds which can add hours to the race if one gets disoriented particularly if there is fog. It was a very productive scouting trip thanks in large part to Dale who was able to show and explain all the problematic areas along the course.

Later on that evening Dale mentioned to Gary that the outfitters that they used to work for on the Moose River were looking for river guides. Dale made it clear that it would be great for them to be able to work together again. Dale added that the outfitter would not hesitate to hire him based on Gary's past experiences there. Dale even offered to Gary his guest house for him to live while he was working the river. No doubt there was a quick surge of adrenaline coursing through Gary at the mere mention of guiding again. But this was neither the time, nor the place to be discussing this when the biggest race of his life was only a couple of days away. Not to be rude, Gary just simply dismissed the idea and suggested that he would talk to Dale about it after the race.

The following day consisted of the sprint trials where the canoe teams paddled downstream then upstream to determine their starting positions for the marathon. Gary and Blake had not been able to practice sprints so they did not have high expectations for the outcome. In fact, their sprint time was only good enough for 45th. They had learned another hard lesson, that short choppy strokes don't work going upstream in shallow waters.

The race organizers put on a pre- race pasta dinner for the race teams. It was a well attended event as over 400 racers, families and fans showed up to honor previous champions and acknowledge the current race participants. Dale invited Gary, Blake, Jennifer, and Chelsea to a large corporate reception where Gary and Blake were interviewed repeatedly by both print and radio reporters. Blake had been taken back by all the attention he was getting, not ever feeling like a celebrity before. He certainly realized that this whole event was a much bigger deal than he realized.

5

Ausable River Canoe Marathon

Before they knew it, race day had arrived and another rough night of sleep for Blake. After breakfast and some last minute adjustments to the boat, Gary insisted Blake get some more shuteye. Later on Gary decided to get some extra sleep of his own being that they were going to be zombies by race time if he didn't. After a late lunch/early dinner, it was time to get the canoe officially measured by racing officials. This inspection was more or less to confirm that the boat was legal (no outboard trolling motors) and to verify the racing class or division they would be racing in.

The next item of business was the mandatory introduction of the paddlers. The introductions were made in reverse order of sprint position; where each team was introduced to the crowd. Needless to say with a 45th place sprint time, Gary and Blake were announced early on. After the singing of several National Anthems, a prep band performance, and the raising of flags, it was time to head to the starting line.

By 8:50 pm, Gary and Blake moved into their assigned position in the street to wait for the start of the race. At precisely 9:00 pm the gun went off and yet another exciting adventure for Gary and Blake was underway. They quickly hoisted their canoes onto their shoulders and ran to the starting point on the river four blocks away. It was quite a site to see as they ran through a sea of paddlers, boats, dropped paddles, and the maddening roar of over 15,000 fans. The scene was chaotic as they passed a few boats on the run; then entered the river in the backwash of some 50 boats and passed a few who had dropped equipment. The Au Sable River is wide as it moves toward Oscoda, but in Grayling, it's less than 20 feet across. Try to imagine 50 canoes and 100 paddlers entering the river, jockeying for position and trying to avoid getting hurt or hurting someone. It is one of the most dangerous race starts anywhere.

The first hour was a wild sprint past thousands of spectators on the riverbank, through cuts and stumps until darkness slowed the pace. Throughout the night Gary and Blake traded positions with some of the slower boats at the back of the pack. It was clear that they could not sustain a strong consistent pace to keep up with even the intermediate boats. They tried to maintain a 70 to 80 paddle stroke per minute pace; but after 50 or so miles, they slowed to about 50 to 60 strokes. During the night they flipped the canoe twice, broke the bow light, lost a paddle and were briefly lost once. The highlight of the race through the night was the flawless performance of Chelsea and Jennifer. They were strategically positioned at every stop to hand over all necessary fluids, food, etc. making the race much more tolerable for Gary and Blake. During one of the dumps into the water, the canoe received an 18 inch gash to the middle bottom. While in the water, they watched their spare paddle and Kevlar repair kit swoosh downstream with the current. After struggling to the next stop they were able to obtain some duct tape from Chelsea and patched the cut as best they could.

Daylight brought on severe sleepiness which Blake cured with caffeine tablets while Gary chose to dwell in his own world for a couple of hours. They struggled through the ponds and portages as a light rain descended through the morning. After reaching Foote Pond the largest and last of the lakes and hours behind the leaders, they encountered strong headwinds, waves and powerboats. Their pain and exhaustion was much more intense than what they experienced in the previous race. Once they saw the finish line they did all they could to push through the pain and aching muscles to cross the line in 41st place. After 18 hours 47 minutes (13 minutes before the cut off time), with a multitude of spasms, cramps, headaches, a bruised ego and a lot of humble pie; they were relieved to have finished the longest canoe race in the world. (The winning team finished with a time of 14:36.) Although they thought for hours that they were the last boat on the river, they were gratified when a Canadian team that they had passed early in the race; finished 20 minutes later. All in all, it was an experience that they would never forget.

In looking back, their last spill in the river could have been disastrous with damage to the boat and sub 40 degree water temperatures. Perhaps this was the most critical point in the race as Blake had become scared and close to hypothermia after being in the water for an extended period of time. He told Gary that he wanted to quit. Gary agreed that they could quit, but not in the middle of nowhere in the dark. Gary knew they had to keep paddling until they saw their pit crew. Once they saw Chelsea and Jennifer at the next pit area, they started feeling better.

They knew that there were a lot of things that could have gone wrong over that many hours and at night. This only further validated their accomplishment. It was clear that Blake and Gary trusted each other and knew that if anything went wrong, they would take care of each other before they would abort the race.

After the last pit stop (more of a pause really), Chelsea and Jennifer drove down to the campground near the finish line to set up camp. But after seeing the physical condition of Gary and Blake at the pit stop, they felt it was more prudent for them to reserve a motel room. Jennifer noticed that while at the stop Gary could not understand or even respond to simple small talk. They were both wincing in pain and Blake was doing everything he could to fight off violent leg cramps. It was clear to Jennifer that they were physically and mentally spent. Gary and Blake were going to need a lot of ice, aspirin, and a good night sleep in a nice comfortable bed to help them recoup for the long drive home on the next day.

6

Opportunity Arises

The next morning before leaving, they ran into Dale Quinn who happened to be staying at the same motel. After discussing battle scars and stories from the previous day marathon, Dale emphatically reiterated to Gary about the possibility of guiding on the Moose. "You were born to do this" and "the river canyons are calling your name" Dale said to Gary." I don't know" Gary said, "that was so long ago and I haven't navigated that kind of water in years". While packing the Suburban, Jennifer overheard the tail end of the conversation and belted out a stern "No way Dale, he's not interested. He has a young family to raise. I absolutely refuse to raise our kids by myself. Plus I have a honey-to-do list a mile long that needs to be completed." Gary and Dale just laughed, shook hands and promised each other to keep in touch. Just as Gary entered the Suburban Dale shouted out one more time, "I mean it Gary, the river is yours for the taking and you know deep down inside that you want it." Gary thought to himself as he was starting the Suburban that Dale hasn't changed much since the last time they met. Dale seemed to be as relentless as ever Gary thought.

Throughout the trip back home, Gary could not clear his mind of Dale's persistence of getting him back to the Moose. Especially his departing last words of "it's your river", and "take the river". Gary knew deep down inside that no one on this planet was going to take The Moose River. It was not for the taking. But there was a little voice in Gary's head that said to go after it, feel alive again, and do what you can to tame it. These thoughts would stay with Gary for a long time.

After getting back home to Montana, life soon became tedious and mundane. Gary was back to his plumbing work but it was a struggle at times dealing with customers who were never satisfied. The passion he once had for it, had been long gone and now he was simply going through the motions.

The best part about it was the fact that he was an independent contractor and didn't have to answer to anyone, except of course the customer. Gary and Blake would occasionally enter races on weekends to break up the monotony, but overall he felt something was missing. Gary couldn't let go of Dale Quinn's last statement to him before leaving The Au Sable River race. Not a day went by where Gary didn't think of the adrenaline rush and excitement that came along with guiding a group down The Moose. He felt guilty with these obsessive thoughts, knowing that it was taking his focus away from his wife and kids. Jennifer had a strong sense that Gary was pondering the opportunity Dale had offered him. She would occasionally see him looking at pictures from his guiding days. She realized that the chance for Gary to guide again was paramount to his happiness. It was obvious to her that he needed this. So it was no surprise to Jennifer when he finally opened up to get her feedback and opinion. He was surprised to see that she was okay with the whole idea and reaffirmed to him that it was his passion and heart and that he needed to follow it. She was not happy or comfortable with the liability involved, but she knew that it was not going to be healthy to hold him back either. They both lightened up the conversation by addressing the fact that they would be out of each other's hair for three months.

Gary decided to call Dale to pick his brain more on the guide positions available and to inform him that he would like to give it a shot. After the conversation with Dale, he was more fired up than ever, and couldn't wait until May when the season begins. During the conversation Dale had inquired about Blake possibly guiding trips as well. Dale was aware of Blake having little experience on turbulent whitewater but was open and comfortable to Gary training him and bringing him up to speed. Gary questioned Dale on the formal administrative paperwork (application process) needed to obtain the job. Dale just laughed and said don't worry about it; it's all been taken care of. After discussing the offer to Blake, it was clear to Gary that Blake did not share the same excitement and enthusiasm that he had. Gary understood and informed Blake that if he ever had a change of heart, the offer would still be available to him.

As time got closer for Gary to start his river-guide work, he had a strong wave of guilt flood his body. He felt that his desire to guide on the Moose was coming across as selfish and irresponsible. He had yet to complete his honey-to-do list that Jennifer had requested of him. The kids will be getting out of school while he was going to be almost 2,000 miles away playing on a river. He ensured them that he would be home in July and that he would call home every other night to talk to them and mommy.

   Dale informed Gary that he would need to get up to Whitehorse a couple of weeks before the season started so that he could scout and train on the river. Gary knew that it was going to take at least two or three runs to reacquaint himself to the river. He would also have to get certified in First Aid –CPR and retrain on all rescue strategies and techniques that are required by the company. The excitement Gary was feeling as time came close; was at times unbearable and he could not wait for his first run to shake out all the butterflies. After saying his goodbyes to Jennifer and the kids, he gave one last pitch to Blake on coming up to The Yukon. Blake appreciated the offer but felt the timing was not right. His relationship with Chelsea had become hot and heavy plus work was not going to allow him a three month hiatus.

7

Reigniting the Passion

Dale picked Gary up at the airport and gave him a little reorientation tour of the area. Gary felt like a kid again as he became giddy recognizing landmarks that he had been so familiar with in his previous trips in and out of Whitehorse. There was no time to waste as they would do a training run the next day on the upper headwaters of the Big Salmon River. Dale felt that the Big Salmon and The Moose have similar hydraulics but that the Big Salmon would be a much tamer river overall to do a training run, plus it was much closer to Dale's home.

Gary was grateful to Dale for presenting him with this opportunity and for reigniting his passion for whitewater. The training run went well as Dale exposed Gary to as much whitewater features as possible, without the severe Class IV and above rapids. The real test was going to be running the much more violent and turbulent Moose. The next few days would be spent settling into Dale's guest house and attending First Aid and CPR classes. After several days of nasty Yukon weather to include high winds and snow, they decided to do a 10 mile section of the Moose in the standard PVC whitewater raft that they will be using for their guiding trips. As they quietly drifted down the swirling Moose River, they couldn't help seeing magnificent Bald Eagles soaring in the canyon. Gary could see the beauty around him, including a waterfall crashing from a nearby bluff; but couldn't appreciate it. The river's enormous flow created traveling whirlpools, eight to ten feet wide, which would appear out of nowhere, swallowing boats up ahead, disappearing and then reappearing farther downriver. Gary and Dale paddled along, and all of a sudden they would feel the river boil* beneath them. Gary began to panic and hyperventilate as he heard Dale scream, "paddle! Paddle harder!" it was too late to recover as the river yanked the bow and flipped Gary out of the raft. Dale was able to quickly turn the stern over to Gary for him to grab hold of Dale's outstretched paddle. It was a close call and lucky for Gary there weren't any boulders or whirlpools to get sucked into.

The Moose was flowing at nearly 80,000 cubic feet per second, almost five times bigger than the Colorado River normally runs. On paper it was exactly the kind of high stakes paddling Gary was yearning for. Gary knew he was rusty but these kinds of things happen to the best river runners. After all Gary asked for this and he got it. Gary knew that this was exactly what made him feel alive.

But the Moose was in fact, meaner, fiercer, and more treacherous than what Gary ever remembered. On later training runs they got sucked into various hydraulics. Even Dale found the river to be more turbulent than in previous years. In fact, Dale proposed to the rafting company that certain sections such as the ones him and Gary experienced were much too risky to run with inexperienced clients. So revisions were made to the guide routes and if need be, a portage would have to be executed.

In early June which was about a quarter into the season, Gary received a phone call from Blake checking to see how things were going. Gary could sense from the tone of the conversation that Blake was not in a good place. He had a major falling out with his employer and decided to become an independent contractor with his physical therapy license. His relationship with Chelsea had become stagnant and didn't seem to be heading in a positive direction. Blake admitted that he missed the canoe racing competitions and the camaraderie that was established between him and Gary competing in the marathons. It was clear that Blake needed a change and told Gary that if there was still room for another guide, that he would be available. The pay wouldn't be great for a novice, but lodging was basically taken care of thanks to Dale.

8

A Team Again

Most of what was left of the season was more or less an apprenticeship for Blake. He first worked one on one with Gary to get acclimated to all the trouble spots along the river. Once Gary felt that Blake was comfortable and obtained the necessary skills, he allowed him to take charge of the trips. After the completion of Gary's tutelage it was time for Blake to show Dale that he was indeed ready to run a trip solo. Once Dale was satisfied with Blake's ability and performance, he allowed him to run a few trips on his own. For only working whitewater for a short period of time, Dale was impressed with Blake's technical ability in reading the river, paddling technique, and spotting problems such as strainers, whirlpools, hydraulics, effective use of eddy's, etc. However, Dale observed early on that when the water got bigger the less Blake would communicate. Effective communication is vital when the water becomes turbulent, especially when you have a group of inexperienced rafters. After everything was said and done, Blake was only able to lead three trips on his own, before the end of the season.

The next season was more of the same except that Blake arrived with Gary to work the full three months. During their off days they would spend time climbing, hiking, fishing; you name it, they did it. In addition, they spent time running the river in solo kayaks, tandem kayaks, canoes, inflatable rafts, dories, and drift boats. It was a man's paradise and both of them couldn't get enough of it.

After arriving to work one morning they heard disturbing news that one of the guides, Steven Sato was killed the previous day leading a small group through the Eagle Canyon section of the Moose. Early reports suggested that Steve was whipped out of the raft from a powerful whirlpool. He became trapped under a large boulder in the Iron Curtain rapid. This is a nasty Class IV rapid that is notoriously known for causing havoc. The under current was so strong that it forced him under and pinned him to the boulder. Apparently the impact of Steve slamming into the boulder knocked him unconscious causing him to drown. Gary and Blake knew him from training sessions and meetings, but Dale knew him best as they had worked together for the past five years. It was tough for Dale to deal with and he was visibly shaken by the news. For the remainder of the season, Dale was not his positive up-beat self. At the conclusion of the guiding season, Dale informed Gary and Blake that he might not guide next year, and felt that he had flirted with peril long enough. Dale insisted that they come back next year to guide and that they would always have a place to stay. It was tough to leave Dale at such a difficult time as he clearly had not gotten past the death of Steve Sato.

During the past guiding season several river guides suggested to Gary and Blake that they should enter next year's Yukon 1000 canoe race. Most of the guides had known that Gary and Blake had previously raced in canoe marathons and felt that this race had their name written all over it. They both had heard about the 1000 before, but never seriously gave it any thought. The race usually takes place near the end of July which would work out good for them as it would not interfere with the river guide season. The Yukon 1000 is the longest paddling race in the world. The race starts on the Yukon River near Whitehorse, Yukon, and ends 1000 miles downriver at a remote Alaska pipeline/Dalton Highway crossing near Fairbanks. The race crosses the Arctic Circle twice. Needless to say, The Yukon 1000 is the pinnacle of canoe marathon races. A paddler looking to enter this race will be looking at six to eight days and 18 hours of solid paddling. The notion of paddling 1000 miles over a week's time seemed too absurd for Gary and Blake. They looked at this race as some kind of publicity or public relations event.

After their season ended guiding the river they became overwhelmed with curiosity and decided to check out the Yukon 1000. Under normal circumstances they would never ever be seen watching a canoe race, they would instead be the ones being watched. However, they were intrigued on how the race was set up and the way they conducted it. Race officials and leaders provided the framework of the race; safety measures, timing, monitoring and communication of teams progress and race position. Essentially each team will need to think of themselves as a self sufficient expedition. It was definitely a different and unique approach to running a race. Gary and Blake felt it was important to leave the Yukon with an open mind when it came to guiding the river next season and the possibility of entering the world's longest canoe race. They left for home on a good note knowing that they had another safe as well as successful season behind them and the opportunity to continue to up the ante of adventure in their lives.

It was April and another adventure was in store for Blake as he was going to marry Chelsea. It had been a long bumpy road to get to this point for both of them. In many ways the time spent apart during the river guide seasons had really solidified their relationship. The only true caveat for Blake in all of this was that he had to promise Chelsea that he would only guide two more seasons. The ultimatum was clear, either it would be Chelsea or it would be the river. They had been through a lot and Blake realized that Chelsea was the real deal. She had the patience and tolerance of a saint and he knew that he would never be able to find someone as wonderful as Chelsea. He assured her that two more years working on the river would be it – no more.

After the wedding they ventured off to Seattle to hop onboard an Alaskan cruise for their honeymoon. Ironically the cruise line offered shore excursions that toured many areas of the Yukon Territory that Blake was familiar with. Chelsea was always envious of Blake spending time in that region and wanted to be able to see for herself how breathtaking the landscape was. It was certainly a part of the world that Blake had become extremely fond of and was excited to know that he would be back within a couple of weeks to begin another season of commercial river guiding. Shortly after arriving back from the cruise, Gary informed Blake that he and Dale had a productive phone call regarding the upcoming season. Near the end of the conversation Dale decided that he would come back to guide another season. Gary felt good after their talk. Dale's decision to come back for another season should help him move on from what had happened to Steve.

At a final get together before heading to the Yukon, both Jennifer and Chelsea learned the possibility of Gary and Blake staying an additional two weeks after the season. They just shook their heads with synchronizing sighs. Much to Gary's chagrin Blake let the cat out of the bag by suggesting that they might enter a 1000 mile canoe race. Simultaneously, Jennifer and Chelsea shuttered with Chelsea uttering "oh great! Something else for us to worry about"! Gary quickly quipped that this is all premature and that there is nothing to worry about. It may never happen and if it does we will let you know if we decide to race. Jennifer questioned them on the need for a pit crew. They were quick to suggest that pit crews are not allowed. Each team must be self sufficient and will need to be fluent in wilderness survival training (fire starting, building shelter, fishing, hunting, water etc.). The men's response did not ease their worries or concerns in any way. But in the end Jennifer and Chelsea just shrugged it off as pure macho madness.

9

Adventure and Its Side Effects

The new season started rather ominously as many guides had been coming back after their trips complaining of major river obstructions coming from downed trees and large debris being backed up into strainers. They felt that the river was not previously cleared or scouted appropriately. Two of the more seasoned guides had clients sustain injuries from their rafts capsizing in and around these obstructions. Two clients in particular had to be taken to a Whitehorse hospital to be treated for concussions and lacerations. The rafting company could not afford to have incidents such as this happen. The image and reputation of the company was at stake. The morale amongst the guides was not good and Dale in particular was agitated. Dale volunteered along with Gary and Blake to do a reconnaissance of the river to ensure a clear unobstructed route for the rafts. They received information from the Canadian Park Service that the snowfall from the previous winter was at an all time high. This was causing major flood conditions along the Yukon and Moose Rivers. The bottom line was that the rafting company would cease all tour operations until the river was deemed to be safe and navigational. This could potentially mean a delay in operations and revenue for up to two weeks.

Early on it was clear from the reconnaissance team that the amount of work to be done was significant. They would need assistance from the Park Service and other rafting companies. The work was going to be dangerous because getting access to the downed trees meant having people situated in the middle of the river, battling strong violent current to cut the limbs without losing their footing. The project was going to demand a multi disciplinarian team with crews along the riverbanks with safety ropes and other equipment. Work crews in watercraft would need to be accompanied by safety personnel. It was going to be labor intensive with a vast amount of resources required. It was going to take an all encompassing collaboration of skill and hard work.

The area of the river that had the highest priority was the Fishing Hook rapid where most of the debris and tree limbs had been collecting – causing a natural dam. The Fishing Hook was a gnarly Class IV* (in some cases Class V* based on water volume) rapid that from above looked like a fishing hook. The rapid was considered by the Park Service to be the third most technically demanding section of the river. It had claimed three lives over the last ten years and caused numerous injuries. At the top of the hook the water current is so strong that it forces watercraft to the outside. This makes it extremely difficult to turn inside (to the left); which is where paddlers need to go in order to avoid boulders and low hanging trees that are on the outer riverbank (right side of the river).

Crews were perplexed on how to resolve the mess that they saw when they arrived. There was no access for them to bring in heavy equipment to assist in the removal of the large tree limbs. All work was going to have to be performed from the riverbanks. The current was much too violent and turbulent to consider having anyone in the river working on the obstructions. In addition, the work was going to have to be done by hand with hand saws, chain saws etc. A Park Service employee who had been cutting limbs along the muddy bank slipped and fell into the unforgiving current. It was a terrifying scene as the rest of the crew looked on in horror knowing that there was nothing that they could do. There were several crews spread out along the river working but this particular crew was the furthest downstream. The team leader radioed safety crews downstream to prepare for a rescue. Safety ropes and floating blocks were strategically thrown into the river hoping that the victim would be able to grasp and subsequently be pulled to safety. The bad news kept coming as it was clear to the safety crews that when the victim zoomed past them he appeared to be unconscious and could not respond to any visual or verbal commands. The body was eventually recovered approximately four miles downstream. It became evident from all of the head wounds sustained that the victim had been knocked unconscious; slamming into the many jagged boulders, shortly after slipping into the river.

The river had claimed yet another victim and with no doubt casted a black shadow over the commercial rafting industry in the region. For the second year in a row the rafting company had to make modifications to their existing routes. The trips would be shortened by at least a mile and a half. Two additional portages were implemented to avoid hazardous sections such as the Fishing Hook. It was common knowledge to any river rat that rivers are dynamic and can change drastically on a daily basis. This was especially true with the Moose River.

The revisions to the river paid off for all concerned. There was positive feedback coming from client evaluation forms and the morale of the guides had drastically improved. It now was a safer river to run in a commercial setting.

Many guides including Gary, Blake and Dale spent their off days running the more challenging river sections that were off limits to guided trips. Often times they would run the river with wooden drift boats or dories. These boats were usually a lightweight boat with high sides, a flat bottom and sharp bows. They are versatile and easy to build because of their simple lines. In fact, during the winter months Dale kept busy building drift boats and selling them to local outfitters who liked to use them for smaller more customized group trips (no more than two or three clients at a time). Dale built his boats with flared topsides to prevent waves coming on board, and extensive built-in buoyancy/storage areas with water-resistant hatches to shed water and keep the boat afloat in the event of a capsize. Dale also built additional special features such as strong rowlocks, long oars, and long blade oars to operate in the highly aerated waters in rapids.

In a drift or dory boat the rower faces down river so that he or she can see the rapids, rocks and hydraulic obstacles. In a rapid the oars are often used to steer the boat as well as to propel it. The speed of running the river in a dory or drift boat is much faster than the rafts. Certainly rowing in a drift boat was a much different experience than paddling in a raft or a whitewater kayak and canoe. For that reason, Gary and Blake loved it and took advantage of any free time they had to run it on the Moose. In fact whenever there was a client(s) who requested to run the river in a dory, Gary or Blake would be the first to volunteer.

After a trip into Whitehorse, Gary and Blake noticed canoeists paddling on the Yukon River reminding them that if they were to enter the Yukon 1000 they better do it soon. It was already at the midway point into the guiding season meaning the Yukon race was only a month and a half away. Both knew that if they entered the race, they would have to dedicate every free moment outside of work to training.

It was a tough decision to stop play boating cold turkey on their off time, but they knew deep down inside they were wired for the Yukon race. The race was yet another plateau to attain on their continuous climb for high adventure. Even the rafting company encouraged them to enter the race as they would sponsor them and help them offset some of the costs.

After registering for the race they contacted their wives via speaker phone to let them know of their plans. When waiting for a response all they heard was awkward silence and a heavy sigh at the end. Jennifer communicated her dismay and was disappointed that they didn't converse with them first before entering the race. Jennifer asked them "what's next?" and "when is this desire for craziness going to end?"

Shortly after talking with Jennifer, Gary received a phone call from the owner of the rafting company. He said that there was an accident on the thumbnail section of the river causing several paddlers to be injured. Dale was in critical condition with fractured ribs, collapsed right side lung and a fractured arm. Gary and Blake rushed to the hospital to see Dale only to be told that visitors were not going to be allowed until the next day. It was a long night for both Gary and Blake with little sleep to be had. By the time they showed up the next day to visit, Dale's condition had deteriorated as he had contracted pneumonia overnight. The mood was quiet and somber with indications strong that Dale might never guide a trip down the river again. The season continued without Dale and the company was now operating with four less guides than what they started the year with. This meant that the remaining guides would now have to work extra hours and days to make up for the loss of staff members. The extra work time now required was going to reduce critical training time for Gary and Blake for their Yukon 1000 preparation.

During one of the many visits to see Dale, the inevitable became a reality as Dale officially retired from river guiding. Although the doctors told him that he would make a full recovery, his head and heart were no longer vested in leading groups on the river. His passion and desire had been wading for quite a while; but the death of Steve Sato combined with his accident placed him in retirement mode.

10

Another Variable to the Equation

During one of Blake's last river runs of the season, he met a filmmaker by the name of Nathan Garner. Mr. Garner was in the area to make a documentary on the Yukon 1000 and other extreme sports. Garner is a TV producer and photo journalist for a Seattle, Washington television station. While in the area, he decided to sign up for a whitewater trip on the Moose River and ended up on a raft trip that Blake was guiding. Blake was impressed with Nathan's adventure resume. He had hiked both the

Pacific Crest Trail and the Appalachian Trail before the age of 23. In high school he took up rock climbing, which led to successfully summiting both Mount Rainier and Denali. If that wasn't enough, he was on the cover of Time Magazine after climbing Mount Everest, Peak number six in a successful seven summits bid (highest peaks on each of the seven continents). A good day in the life of Nathan Garner would most likely include scuba diving, skiing, sky diving, climbing, biking and running. He would like to add adventure whitewater boating, or extreme river paddling to the mix. Of course, all of these things make for great television or movie drama and it was clear that Nathan was searching for his next blockbuster production.

After the trip with Blake they spent a good deal of time exchanging adventure stories. He asked Blake if he wouldn't mind showing him a few whitewater techniques in a drift boat on his next available trip. "As long as you are a paying client I can show you everything and anything on that river," Blake said. However, he did explain to Nathan that the only one that would be operating the boat would be himself. He told him the company would fire him on the spot if they found out that he gave the reigns of the boat to a client.

The two met up with Gary later that day for dinner to discuss the possibility of Nathan featuring them in his upcoming documentary on the Yukon 1000. They had no objections to it as long as there were no obstacles or obstructions to the process of them completing the race. Nathan picked their brains on what they would face and what they needed to do to have a successful event.

The Yukon 1000, or "Big Empty" as some people call it winds through some of the emptiest land on the continent and racers are expected to carry enough gear and supplies to last for at least two weeks on the water. In addition, the Yukon flows through some of the most isolated grizzly and black bear territory on the continent, making the race a rite of passage.

Gary and Blake explained to Nathan that instead of relying on a small army of volunteers to man checkpoint stations, each team must report its progress using a SPOT (satellite messenger device). This device or personal locator beacon would not only be used for tracking purposes but for emergencies as well. The device consists of a panic button that when touched alerts race officials in case something goes wrong while the team is on the water. They both knew that the Yukon 1000 is all about stamina, perseverance and endurance, not about short sprints. It was going to be vintage survival. To prevent racers from paddling nonstop and running themselves down, each team is required to check in each evening before 11:15pm and stay or camp for at least six hours. They also knew that they were going to have to contend with the rigors of whitewater, fallen trees, boulders, strainers, and poorly mapped channels where one wrong turn could force competitors to backtrack upstream. Nathan thought to himself that the race seemed like a very fast camping trip. But it seemed to be a compelling camping trip filled with drama, adventure, and intrigue. This would certainly be an event that his viewers or audience would be fascinated with.

Nathan mentioned to Blake and Gary that he would like to check in with them each night of the race to gather details or updates on the day's performance. In addition to Gary and Blake, he was also going to be following other teams in the race to get their insights and perspectives for the documentary.

They began packing up all their food and gear for the Yukon 1000 shortly after the last rafting trip of the season. It took almost a full day to load two zero degree sleeping bags, four season tent, shotgun, 100 lbs of food, maps, a satellite phone, satellite tracking device, GPS, dry-suits, dry bags, mosquito net, compass, stove and fuel, first aid supplies, solar charger and more. After loading the canoe they couldn't help but think that it looked more like a container ship than a racing vessel. But they realized that this race significantly revolved around wilderness survival. Race day had arrived along with anticipation and high anxiety with occasional panic.

11

The Yukon 1000

The gun went off at 11:00am Monday morning, officially starting the Yukon 1000. With the exception of missing a stretch of great campsites, the rest of the day and the six hour camping stop overnight, were uneventful. There was not a lot of drama or excitement to provide Nathan and it wasn't unintentional that they found a camping area that had no access to the outside world. Subsequently Nathan could not check in to get an update from them. This meant that they could focus on getting food and rest without someone asking them questions. It wasn't until the third day into the race that Nathan realized that with the race course being so isolated his only means of access to the racers would be with him actually being on the river with them. This meant that he had to hire a Yukon River guide with a canoe to help him gain access to the racers. He had inadvertently planned on the participants having designated camping areas where he could consistently meet up with them. Gary and Blake had three nights of camping all by themselves. Other than bears, foxes, owls, wolves, and other wildlife there was no one there to pester them. At this point they would rather have the sound of animals interrupting their train of thought than a reporter. Mosquitoes were a problem they could do without, but thanks to their mosquito net, they were able to manage well enough.

By the time Nathan caught up with them it was the fourth night and more than half way into the race. It was a brutal day of paddling for Gary and Blake as they encountered strong headwinds, heavy rain and several unexpected portages; not great timing for them to divulge their inner thoughts and opinions on how the race was going. But they felt bad for Nathan after hearing his struggles in making the documentary and provided what they could to appease him. Nathan had expressed to Gary that he was not happy with what he had compiled for the documentary. So far, all he had was some historical facts on the race, and profiles/bios on several racers, including Gary and Blake. He also had the usual information on past winners and rules and regulations. He had racing updates (locations of teams on the river). He felt he needed something more compelling and riveting; something with more wow factor.

Perhaps his frustration in not having drama or excitement for the documentary was about to change when later in the evening after everybody was asleep a black bear had ransacked their camp. The bear first started eating food that was left out near the canoes. But then became beyond curious after it had consumed all subsistence that was available. The clothes line where they had canopies, tarps, shoes, clothing, blankets, and towels hanging to dry, was torn down with one mighty swipe of its massive paw. The tent where Gary and Blake were sleeping was next in line to become carnage. It was an unmistakable sound for Nathan's guide, as he had experienced this before in previous backcountry guide trips. He promptly yelled out to Gary and Blake to evacuate before they become easy pickens being laid up in a tent. After getting Nathan up he grabbed his shotgun and proceeded to one of the tent windows to visualize the bear. Once he saw Gary and Blake narrowly escape from their tent he unzipped the front door of his tent to see if he had a clear shot. In order to get a lethal shot he was going to have to get out of his tent and position himself to the side. After establishing his position and seeing the bear shredding Gary's tent and sleeping bags he fired twice; killing the bear on the spot.

Nathan confessed to having left food items out creating a dangerous scenario in an area infested with hungry bears. His careless disregard of maintaining a safe environment angered Gary and Blake as well as his own river guide. Much of the wilderness equipment that they had cherished and needed now was damaged beyond repair. Perhaps the most critical equipment damaged in the attack was the GPS receiver that allowed Gary and Blake to be tracked by satellite. Even the panic button located on the receiver was deemed useless, making it impossible to alert race officials that something was wrong. Other items damaged in the melee were river maps, mosquito nets, stove and compass.

The river guide that Nathan hired was disgusted and sad that he had to eliminate such an impressive and amazing creature. He knew that all of this could have been prevented if everyone practiced common sense in a wilderness setting. The remainder of their overnight break was dedicated to assessing all the damage and what if any of the equipment they could salvage. They seriously contemplated on removing themselves from the race. Otherwise they may have to extend their overnight break to recover from all that had happened. Any thought of winning or placing in the top five places was out of the question. They were extremely fortunate that the bear did not do any damage to the canoe or paddles. At this point survival and finishing the race was the ultimate objective. They all knew that they were close to being killed and realized how lucky they were to be alive.

Nathan, still visibly shaken from the incident, suggested to Gary that once he locates a racing official he will explain to them everything that happened. He will convey to the official specific arrival and departure times to and from the campsite. Essentially he would plead to them on their behalf not to disqualify them. With the help of his guide they would verify and validate that there was no violation of the rules and that the situation could not have been avoided.

After extending their stay at the campsite they were still consumed with resentment towards Nathan jeopardizing their race, and their lives. They tried their best to put it behind them as they began paddling on day five. Needless to say they would be more than happy if they never saw Nathan Garner again.

Racing officials realized that there was a potential problem when Gary and Blake had not checked in with their tracking device to signify when and where they stopped and started. Nor did they receive any panic button signal from them. Officials of the race had dispatched a safety boat early in the morning to locate them. Three hours after Gary and Blake departed for day five, Nathan had finally found a race official to fill him in on what had happened.

Gary and Blake did all they could to keep their eyes open after only three hours of sleep. Reading the river was extremely difficult and tension was building between the two. Without river maps and a compass they were praying that there wouldn't be any forks in the river to throw them off. They were going to concentrate on paddling wherever the most volume of water was flowing. Following this logic is dangerous especially when there is similar current on either side of the river and multiple strainers or sweepers* located throughout the course.

Day five consisted of the fastest water current they had seen for the race. With all that had occurred overnight they somehow paddled over 153 miles far into Alaska. They were both in a zone that they have never experienced before. Perhaps it was a combination of anger, frustration, determination, perseverance and a lot of adrenaline. Either way it was the most productive day they have ever had on a body of water. A day that they could have easily given up and said no more, we are done. They were too exhausted to acknowledge any of this and the impact that all of this would have on their confidence and psyche. It appeared that they were more motivated than ever. However, chills flooded their bodies near the end of the day when they saw several black bears along the riverbank as they were looking for a camping spot. As tired as they were they knew that they were going to have to be vigilant as ever in finding a safe camping location.

Without a tent they would have to improvise shelter by building a lean-to*. They did everything they could to reinforce the open side section of the lean-to. Boulders, limbs, vinyl from their damaged tent and even their canoe were situated to give them a barrier between them being in the lean-to and any wildlife. No longer having a stove to cook their food they had to rely on Meals Ready to Eat (MRE's) and dehydrated foods that they had brought along. They agreed to take shifts watching for bear activity but that idea quickly vanished as exhaustion took over. After eight hours of hard sleeping they prepared the boat for day six. Gary felt that they still had another 250 miles to go. But with good weather and fast current, he figured that they could finish up within the next two days.

The most technical portions of the race course took place on day six. A major portion of day six was spent paddling through several canyons with sharp turns and nasty whitewater. They encountered numerous strainers, undercuts, and even recirculating holes* (sometimes pull boaters under the water and hold them in place). On one occasion they had come upon a boat that was pinned against some downed logs. They knew that the boat was in the race because it had the current Yukon 1000 logo and race number in the designated right front location. There were no paddlers to be found. They decided to pull into a nearby eddy* to assess the situation. It was distressing to them not knowing what had happened. No longer having their panic button they had no way to signal to race organizers that there was an emergency. They didn't see anything in the water that would suggest a drowning plus the water wasn't deep enough to sustain a drowning. After several minutes of investigating they decided to move on and hoped that the paddlers safely exited the boat. They cringed at the thought of possibly seeing the paddlers' lifeless bodies floating downstream.

It was another day of fast current and when they finally decided to pull the boat out they had paddled around 120 miles. After setting up yet another lean-to and eating what was left of their dehydrated foods for dinner they couldn't help reflecting on the past present and future. They were confident that if everything went well they would be able to paddle the remaining 130 miles and finish the race.

The fact that race organizers and officials could no longer track them on the river without their GPS, Gary and Blake assumed that they were officially out of the race. Perhaps in the eyes of the Yukon 1000 organizers, Gary and Blake were doing this in vain, but to them this race was still alive and well and in their minds, this was the real deal. Little did they know that Nathan had presented a case to the organizers on their behalf to maintain their eligibility in the race. He stepped up to the plate to keep them an active participant in the race. The officials would have to take Gary and Blake's word on whether they were taking their required six hour overnight break.

They still had no idea what position they were in and they didn't really give a hoot. They hadn't seen a human being in almost two days and began to wonder if there was anybody out there. They remember passing two teams on day three but believed several teams passed them while camping on day four. Possibly even more teams passed them the night of day five after they took an additional two hours to recover.

Throughout the overnight break they did everything they could to fend off mosquitoes. Not having their beloved mosquito net meant no protection, thus making it open season for mosquito bites. This gave them yet another motivating factor to get back out on the water and to move on towards the finish.

It was a sluggish start to day seven as they were both mentally and physically worn out. Gary was experiencing excruciating shoulder pain and other aches while Blake was having both shoulder and back pain. Lactic acid had taken over their bodies as both suffered from constant muscle cramps and spasms. They both had bad colds and it was only to get worse as they began paddling in a monsoon. Unlike the previous two days where the current was fast, this day was slow and flat. It was like paddling on a large wide open lake with a lot of wind in the face. The flat water with headwind was brutal and it was slowing them down drastically. Turning the boat was like turning a barge. They had to paddle extra strokes to avoid downed trees and limbs that were blocking their direct line of travel. There were no chutes or shortcuts to paddle through. They knew that the finish line was relatively close as they could feel the heat coming off of the Alaskan pipeline. At this point nothing was going to stop them and the closer they got to the finish the more they dug hard to get there.

12

A Feat to Be Proud Of

Another milestone had been reached as they paddled across the finish line. A surge of pride and exaltation went through their bodies as they heard their names announced over the loud speakers. Their bodies collapsed with exhaustion by the time they reached the take-out* point. While race volunteers assisted them in pulling the canoe out of the water they could hear Dale yelling congratulatory remarks nearby. It was a pleasant surprise to hear Dale's voice welcoming them at the finish line. He was not expected to be there until the next day when he was to transport them back to Whitehorse. Dale drove the 588 miles up to Fairbanks a couple of days earlier to deliver one of his custom handmade drift boats to a local outfitter. After the delivery he drove to the finish line area to cheer them on. Even Dale heard about the bear attack through conversations with some of the race volunteers.

It was great to have Dale there and to see that he had made a full recovery from his injuries. The three friends gathered together for a group hug and later posed for some final race photos taken by a local newspaper photographer.

They found out later that the canoe they saw trapped in a strainer was the result of an overcorrection and the canoe becoming sideways. The location was so isolated and inaccessible the paddlers had to be plucked out of the river by a local fire and rescue helicopter. The panic button located on the GPS tracking device that was provided to all the racers proved to have saved their lives. All they knew at this point was that one paddler was in serious condition with spinal injuries and the other was in critical condition with head trauma.

Several media outlets interviewed both Gary and Blake on the race but most of the questions pertained to the bear attack. They were asked what place they came in and all they could do was look at each other and shake their heads. A race volunteer nearby overheard the question and quickly interjected that they were the twelfth team to come in and that there were four teams still out on the race course. Up to this point there were eight teams that had pulled out of the race. The bottom line was they had accomplished a tremendous feat and would be proud of it forever.

Later on one, of the race organizers mentioned to Gary that Nathan explained everything to them and that he presented a compelling case to keep them active in the race. The potential risk of what happened to them or to any other racer was always present and unfortunately the precedent was established by Gary and Blake. Nathan expressed to them that it was him that created and caused a dangerous environment by leaving food out. The officials decided based on evidence provided by Nathan that they would make an exception to the rule book and keep Gary and Blake officially in the race. Gary expressed his gratitude to the official for understanding and recognizing their racing achievements. A race organizer later told Gary that with the race being relatively new, nothing like this had ever happened before. It took the experiences of Gary and Blake to force them to reexamine safety measures and other rules and regulations for future races. As it turned out, the news of their bear attack became the top news story of the race. Everybody seemed to know about it and essentially they had become instant celebrities because of it.

They would spend the next two nights in a local motel to recover and to attend a post race recognition event on the second night. By then all racers would have completed their races. At the event they met up with Nathan to thank him for presenting and explaining all the details to the race officials. They appreciated him for making it possible for them to be legitimate racing participants in the eyes of the racing rules committee.

Nathan asked if it would be alright if he could get one more interview and some final thoughts to add to his documentary. Blake gave Nathan his contact information and invited him to come back next season for more instruction on navigating boats down the Moose. Nathan was grateful for the offer and informed him that he would send a copy of the documentary when it is finished. Before departing for the night he asked them to contact him before they went onto their next venture. He assured them that he would not get in their way and would love to provide a medium or outlet to relay/communicate their exciting adventures to the general public. Nathan expressed that there was a large demand or market for viewing programs that featured thrilling adventures and people who live life on the edge. He would certainly love to be an active participant in providing this type of programming to the thrill-seeking public. He apologized for the bear incident, shook their hands and asked them to keep in touch.

After spending a few additional days with Dale in Whitehorse it was time for their triumphant return home. Perhaps all that had happened throughout the guiding season and the close calls during the Yukon 1000 made them extremely homesick. They realized how precious life was and couldn't wait to hug their loved ones.

It was definitely a family affair when they arrived at the airport. Jennifer and the kids with Chelsea and other friends greeted them at the gate with, signs "Welcome home daddy", "Congratulations Gary and Blake", "You did it". It was very uplifting for them and they were overwhelmed with emotions. Their emotions were on full display as they smiled, laughed and shed lots of tears. They hugged their wives like they never had before.

They were grateful to be home safely with their family and friends. This time being home was so much more special and gratifying. Even getting back to work in making a living was welcomed with open arms. They were emotionally drained from the past season and felt the need to be grounded again. It was essential for them to savor every waking moment with their families. Just about every weekend, right up to the end of autumn, they all got together to go camping. If they weren't camping they were picnicking together or taking the kids to the zoo. Chelsea and Blake had become a sort of surrogate aunt and uncle to Gary's children. Gary and Jennifer often times felt that Chelsea and Blake looked more like the natural parents of their children then they did. They were great with the kids and no doubt would be terrific parents of their own.

Blake received a phone call from Nathan to see how things were going and that he was going to be sending him and Gary a copy of the Yukon 1000 documentary. The documentary was going to be seen on a local Seattle television station as well as most public television stations throughout the country. He was unsure of the nationwide air date but would let them know when the Montana PBS stations would air it. He suggested to Blake to keep an open mind while watching the program and feel free to provide any feedback, negative or positive.

Nathan mentioned to Blake that he would like to do a feature story on commercial guiding on the Moose River. He would like to feature individual guides such as Blake to show the audience or readers the life and times of a river guide on one of the most treacherous rivers in North America. Blake was flattered with the idea and suggested that he would be okay with it. Nathan reminded Blake to inform him of any adrenaline trips in the making. Chelsea overheard the phone conversation with Nathan and it reminded her that Blake had promised to her that the upcoming season would be his last. After his conversation with Nathan he could tell by her facial expressions and body language that she was looking for confirmation that she would no longer have to worry about him getting hurt or possibly killed on the river. He reiterated to her that this would be his last season – no more.

13

The Need for More

Early on in the new year Gary had learned about an old buddy of his who he guided with that executed a record speed run down the Snake River. He had read several stories in the past about guides paddling speed runs on various rivers. Speed runs had been attempted on the Salmon River in Idaho, Tuolumne River in California, Rio Santa Maria in Mexico, Nahatlatch River in British Columbia and of course many runs have been attempted on the Colorado River in Arizona. Gary could not seem to take his mind off of these river runs and before he knew it the wheels were in motion on the thought of him performing a run of his own. He was perplexed on what was happening in his thought process. Only five months ago he was ecstatic to be home. Yet he couldn't stop brainstorming on the next adventure. The feelings of guilt and selfishness came roaring back yet again. He continued to beat himself up internally but kept dwelling on the fact that he knew that he and Blake could pull this off. No one had ever succeeded in performing this on the Moose River nor has anyone attempted it as far as Gary knew. The juices were flowing again and he couldn't wait to tell Blake about his projected plan.

After briefing Blake on the proposed trip Blake was just as excited as Gary had been when researching information on it. It would be an accomplishment that would be highly heralded in the adventure world. But more importantly, their peers would place them on a pedestal that would demand the ultimate respect.

They both agreed that the run would be most likely attempted in early June when the volume of water would be at its most efficient. The attempt would not interfere with their regular commercial guide work schedule as they would only need two full days. This kind of endeavor was illegal in the eyes of the Canadian Park Service and they knew that the rafting company would not approve of such a stunt. They would have to keep a trip like this under wraps and could not allow any information of the trip to leak out.

They spent hours studying Moose River maps highlighting problematic areas and significant river features to include rapids, whirlpools, waterfalls, portages, eddy's, etc. Gary had seen a great deal of the Moose River in previous runs but never paddled the entire route. Blake on the other hand only had experience through the rafting company on maybe 50 of the 200 miles. They looked at calmer sections of the river where they could take a break to eat, drink, and switch rowers. The trip would be executed in a drift boat. This trip would include starting at Harper's Point boating access site to Lake Watson 200 miles downstream. The trip would take them on the full length of the Moose River.

They called Dale to inform him of their plans and to see if he could help them with some of the logistic demands of the trip. The first response from Dale was, "you're nuts! It's far too dangerous and the Park Service would never allow you to do it". Gary told Dale that he had studied the map thoroughly and had a fool proof plan of attack on even the nastiest sections. Dale insisted that they reconsider and forget about it. This however, went over deaf ears and Dale eventually told them that he would help them out. Dale primarily would help transport them and the boat to Harpers Point where they would begin the trip and then at the end pick them up at the boat launch at Lake Watson. He would also try to check in with them at designated access sites to ensure they were alright and if they needed anything. Both of them agreed not to divulge details about the trip to their wives. They would only tell them that it was a customized trip for VIP's that would take two days. No sense giving them something extra to worry about.

During the planning of the trip, Blake had been communicating with Nathan as to what they were planning to do. Nathan was very much interested and suggested that it was important for them to have their trip recorded and documented. Nathan suggested to Blake that in order to create the most personal and most effective documentary, he would have to document everything as an active participant. To create a compelling and most dramatic story he would need to be in the boat with them. He would need to see, hear, feel smell, taste, and touch everything they do. Dale saw this as something the general public and certainly outdoor enthusiasts would enjoy reading or seeing. "Something like this would put you guys on top of the adventure world and it will be critical that people know about it," Nathan said. Blake made it clear that it wasn't himself that needed to buy in on it, it was Gary. Blake told Nathan that Gary was going to be much more guarded and reluctant in agreeing to another documentary. In fact Blake let it all out by saying that Gary was not a big fan of Nathan's aggressive and persistent style of work during the Yukon story. After watching the documentary, Gary felt that Garner embellished certain details and facts about the race that was not accurate and misleading. In essence he felt that Garner was pretty much a media ratings whore and fabricated as much drama to help promote viewership. Specifically he felt that the documentary overdramatized the bear attack depicting that there were more damage and more injuries than what really happened. Gary had heard from other paddlers that Nathan had fabricated health concerns suggesting that certain participants had suffered from severe hypothermia and dehydration. Racing conditions were embellished stating that the water lever of the river was above the banks creating deadly scenarios along the race course. Yes individuals were seriously injured, but it wasn't because of flood conditions. Gary felt that recognition and fame is fine, but it needs to be genuinely earned.

Nathan knew that something was wrong because Gary hadn't returned any of his e-mails. It was going to be a tough sell but Blake told Nathan that he would try his best to help Gary become more comfortable with the idea.

Two weeks before leaving for the upcoming river guiding season, Chelsea announced to Blake that she was pregnant. Blake became airborne with excitement and joy. She was two months pregnant and was going to be due in late November. They celebrated nonstop and vowed to share their great news with everybody at the next picnic. The news solidified even more, Blake's decision to call it quits after the upcoming rafting season. He was on cloud nine along with Chelsea on the knowledge of them becoming parents.

A festive mood was clearly evident at the picnic as Chelsea announced to everybody that she was pregnant. The woman gathered together to discuss the baby and future plans regarding the nursery, baby shower, etc. The men came up to congratulate Blake on the wonderful news and made bets on how soon he would have his son or daughter paddling or rowing in a boat.

Things became more serious later on when Blake sat Gary down to discuss Nathan's proposed documentary. Blake knew that Gary was not on the same page with Nathan, but perhaps they could see eye to eye if all the details of executing the river run and making the documentary of the run were clearly stipulated on paper. Call it a contract if you will, but the bottom line would specifically lay out what was expected of everybody to show where everybody stood. In essence, Nathan would explicitly know what he could or what he could not do.

14

Three's A Crowd

Initially Gary was not at all pleased with the notion of Blake communicating their plans to Nathan and that he was so adamant about having Nathan literally coming on board. Gary felt that Blake had drastically underestimated the technical skills, technique, mental and physical toughness and perseverance required to complete the proposed task. This was going to be a task that someone like a Nathan Garner would have no business participating in. Gary knew all too well that you never ever underestimate a river such as this, and a greenhorn onboard only creates more liability. This would be the most demanding experience that anyone could ever imagine, even for Gary. Gary should know because he had paddled some of the more difficult segments of the Moose River in his previous trip over ten years ago. This endeavor will be an attempt at a speed run down the Moose River in a 14 foot wooden drift boat. This trip will include 200 miles of the most treacherous paddling and unforgiving obstacles that most humans have never seen. Certainly nothing that someone of the likes of a Nathan Garner had ever seen before. Blake further defended Nathan in that if it wasn't for him they might not have been recognized as active participants and official finishers of the Yukon 1000. Blake asked Gary who else showed the level of interest in them and their goals than what Nathan did? Blake suggested that regardless of what Gary thought of him, he genuinely showed interest in them where no one else had.

Gary agreed to talk with Nathan one on one to get his true intentions and find out if there was any hidden agendas. They had a lengthy conversation to include much of what Blake had told him previously. Perhaps Nathan sealed the deal with the suggestion that he would allow Gary to proofread all written words and review all video footage of the documentary before it would be released to the public and all media outlets. He would be an active participant in the entire process, and would have the final say on all content. Essentially, nothing would be released to the public until Gary put his stamp of approval on the product. Nathan was doing everything he could to get Gary's acceptance. With Gary's agreement much of the costs for the project would be offset through several sponsors and the Seattle TV station Nathan worked for.

They eventually agreed to the terms and would arrange for Nathan to arrive several days before the actual trip to teach him many of the fundamentals needed for rowing a drift boat in Class III – IV rapids.

After the conversation with Nathan, Gary felt that he may have sold himself to the devil. He had an uneasy feeling about what had transpired and even felt regret by agreeing to have Nathan participate. Originally this project was to be a straight forward adventure trip with Blake and himself. Now it had become more complicated with additional liability of a third individual with no experience.

Of course, Gary was going to be the leader on this escapade and as mentioned before, he was the ultimate river rat; a compact, supremely fit man with an eccentric streak that was balanced by a thorough knowledge of the mysterious physics of the Moose's notorious rapids. Gary had been a guide on the Moose River for over 10 years so he knew a great deal of the power and skill needed to run it. Gary was confident and positive about Blake who at this point was a superb paddler with a lot of precision and power. The biggest concern about Blake was that he had much less experience in a wooden boat such as a dory where oars are used as opposed to paddling in a canoe or kayak. Outside of training, 3 years of guiding on the Moose and a few races he had limited experience with whitewater rowing. The weakest link by far was going to be Nathan Garner who had the least amount of river miles. His fitness and stamina were strong but his ability to read a river or rowing skills were weak at best. In fact Gary was still not comfortable and was not sleeping well at night with the notion of someone like Nathan Garner being a part of the team.

He still struggled with the fact that the public may view this as more of a publicity stunt than as a professional skilled accomplishment. Gary became even more stressed when realizing the problem of tackling perhaps the toughest and most dangerous 40 mile river stretch in North America. Rowing through the entire length of the Gunnison Canyon unscathed may be an insurmountable task. He knew all too well of the extreme danger that this section of the river presents. He had flashbacks of running this stretch with a drift boat navigating rapids named; Tumble Home, Slaughterhouse, Iron Ring, Devil's Curve, Lost Paddle and Double Z. the difference back then was he ran the canyon solo with no one to rely on or having someone rely on him. The only thing that could hold him back was the river and himself. Gary was the third and last to have successfully run this section. In retrospect he remembered the initial anxiety and the sacrifice of blood, guts, sweat, fear; escaping the canyon by the narrowest of margins. He knew that the river's water volume may dictate what will happen and if portages will be required.

Before they knew it, it was time to head out to the Yukon for the next rafting season. It was another difficult goodbye for them as they each kissed their wives goodbye. Jennifer asked Gary when and what it would take to slow down his ever continuing thirst for thrill and adventure. "You know that you can't keep an eagle from flying" Gary said. Jennifer knew this but was hoping that he would tone it down a bit. While hugging his kids he looked up and saw something in Jennifer's eyes that he hadn't seen before. It was a look of sadness and he felt compelled to ease her mind. He gave her another kiss and hug, telling her not to worry and that this was going to be his last season river guiding. She returned a big smile with tears in her eyes and told him to be safe. After Blake kissed Chelsea's baby belly, he confirmed to her that there will be no more goodbyes and that this was his last rafting season. He promised Chelsea that he would call every night to talk to her and the baby. They hugged again and Chelsea began weeping as they each waved goodbye.

15

The Mighty Moose River

The new rafting season was well underway and both Gary and Blake navigated their respective guide trips without much drama or trouble. Nathan arrived in Whitehorse where he would be staying with Gary and Blake in Dale's guesthouse. Gary took Nathan out on the river the following day to get him exposed to some of the river features they would be facing. All things considered, Nathan performed well and seemed enthusiastic to learn. Gary made it clear to Nathan that the only time he would be rowing during the run would be on the flat, slower flowing section of the river. These sections would be wider and would consist of Class III rapids or less.

The rafting company could only afford Gary and Blake to have the next five days off. The peak of the season was only a week away, so this was the best chance for them to get away. They figured they could get two solid days of work on the river before the actual speed run. Nathan was catching on relatively fast but needed a lot of guidance on reading the river and picking the right line through the rapids.

Considering that they would be rowing at night during the run, they were going to need to get accustomed of rowing through the rapids in darkness. They decided to do a practice run through Rock Canyon which contained difficult Class III – IV sections that would provide a great test for them. The three of them would be wearing headlamps to help them through the darker sections or sections where moonlight was obstructed.

They began rowing around 8:00 pm near Whitmore Bluffs. This section was ideal for Nathan to row because it was calm water. As he rowed, he would pause at the end of every fifth and sixth stroke to glance over his shoulder to gaze downstream, looking for the flush of whiteness that would suggest a rapid. Gary was situated in the bow to give Nathan assistance with running lines. Nathan could distinguish the white caps of the waves as long as the moonlight made it down to the river. It was especially difficult in Rock Canyon where much of the moonlight was obstructed. He was rowing in pitch black darkness forcing him to rely on feeling subtle vibrations that the river sent through the wooden oar shafts into his hands and fingers.

While Nathan was rowing through several Class III rapids, Gary and Blake needed to perform a series of highsiding* techniques to level the boat. It was all about having an instinctive feel for river hydraulics*. While gripping the gunwales* they braced for the oncoming waves with a slight lean of the shoulders or when needed, a thrust of their torsos to maintain the boats balance.

This work however between Blake and Nathan was anything but nonverbal harmony. It was obvious that Nathan was a nervous wreck and Blake had to shout out to him what he needed to do. Often, Blake would look to Gary with a befuddled expression to suggest, what we were thinking to bring Nathan along.

Gary wanted everybody to swap positions in the boat every 15 minutes. When the rower became exhausted he would call for a break, move toward the stern or the bow while his replacement shifted to the rowing position. Only Garner was excluded from this process as he was the least experienced. Plus he would be filming and documenting as much of the trip as possible. Although, whenever there was a stretch of flat-water or any water that was Class III or less, he would take over the rowing duties.

The strategy was to row the drift boat (bow first) forward through the bigger rapids and row backwards through the calmer sections to maximize speed. Normally the order of rowing would be – first Gary then Blake, and then Nathan; depending on river conditions. The order of rowing would more or less remain the same with each crewman circling the decks from rowing position to stern to bow as they moved downstream.

Gary felt that the river that they were rowing on felt much different, strange and thrilling. It is the thrilling and adrenaline part that really was the catapult for both Gary and Blake to take on this endeavor. This potential accomplishment after all, would be by far the pinnacle of both their lives. As far as it goes for Nathan Garner, neither Gary, nor Blake was really sure what to make of Garner's intentions or motives. Up to this point, other than his nervous energy, the extra weight and space needed for his camera gear, he hasn't been too much of a detriment. The commercial rafting companies didn't run trips through Rock Canyon because of its lack of access and location. It had been three years since Gary and Blake last ran it. Rock Canyon was much less challenging than Gunnison Canyon leaving Gary to wonder how intense the Gunnison Canyon section will be. He began to question if they should attempt the speed run. Between Blake and himself they had 13 years of experience on the Moose River. Not exactly an impressive number but enough experience to pull it off. He knew it was an enormous challenge but at the same time, he resented the fact that his confidence seemed to be wavering. Adding to the challenge is the limited whitewater experience of Garner and the risk he brings to the project.

In certain respects, Gary was refreshed to visualize the river in its current wild and wonderful state. For the last 30 years the Moose River had been constrained by a dam giving it a not so natural feel. But with excessive rain and snow from the past winter and spring, the Moose River appeared to be unbound and as natural as ever. As they rowed downstream each of them experienced their own level of thrill and exhilaration. This was going to be the kind of event that Nathan Garner could only dream of. This event would put him into the upper echelon of outdoor photojournalist/ videographer fame. It certainly would be an adventure that no other photo journalist has ever performed or been an active participant of. As far as he knew, this was going to set an industry standard that would be extremely difficult to match.

They finished their 80 mile practice run with much more confidence then what they started with. It was a confidence builder in that they traveled 20 extra miles than originally planned and successfully navigated through several Class IV rapids.

The following day was going to be a day of rest as well as shopping for food, supplies and equipment. They ended the day with the largest carbohydrate consumption any of them had ever had.

16

The Run of Their Lives

The day of reckoning had arrived and there was no shortage of anxiety and excitement. Before setting off on their epic journey, Dale made one last appeal to get them to reconsider. Recently, park rangers had been on high alert due to more than usual rafting activity in the Gunnison Canyon section. Certain sections of the Moose River in the Gunnison Canyon were off limits to boaters and were deemed illegal. There was a time that permits were required but after several tragedies over the years even permits were not granted. The park service looked at these river runs in the canyon as dangerous, irresponsible and flat out dumb. All violators would be prosecuted and face a hefty $15,000 fine. Undermining the authority of the Yukon Park Service had never been a problem for Gary. He had undermined them 10 years ago when he zoomed past their checkpoints on his legendary run through the canyon. He was not a fan of the park service regulating Mother Nature and gifts from the almighty. He remembered the good old days when a person could launch a boat and paddle down river through canyons without having to ask permission. Gary didn't want to hear anymore reasons not to do the trip as he was nervous enough. They discussed final details with Dale on the use of the two-way radio and various logistical issues pertaining to the trip. The radio would be utilized to communicate any emergencies and location updates to Dale.

The trip would begin at Harpers Point, which is where most Moose River runs started. The actual put-in* was located 10 miles below the Miles Canyon Dam which is listed as mile zero on most river maps. The end line was mile 200 at the Whitmore Bluffs, near the entrance to Lake Watson. Before heading out, Dale used Nathan's camera to get video footage of the three of them standing at the starting point (on the bank of the river) and of them sitting in the boat. Dale then helped them position the boat in the river to begin the run. Dale gave them the signal to start. At the same time he started his stop watch as he was going to document and keep track of the amount of time from beginning to end. To get from beginning to end they estimated would require approximately two nights and days of strenuous rowing.

The first part of the trip reconfirmed to Gary what he had learned two days earlier that the river was a whole new animal. The river was showing itself as an ugly monster with ferocious unpredictability. The same day they did their practice run, several guided trips near the entrance of the Gunnison Canyon encountered monster hydraulics. They were unaware of this as well as not knowing that there were several injuries and a fatality as a result. Perhaps had they known about this they might have scratched the trip. Nathan did his best at verbally describing river features while at the same time videotaping their movement on the river. Blake had to correct him several times during his narration of the trip and his use of words in describing the river features. Nathan was still limited in his knowledge of whitewater terminology. He was struggling mightily with his camera as they engaged crashing waves, keeper holes*, drops* and strainers. He did everything he could to maintain control of his $1600 video camera. Up to this point the original plan of having

Nathan row while on calm flat water or Class II* or less had been non applicable. Ever since the boat hit the water it had been a mad scramble. There had not been a stretch of calm water since the start. And with them entering the Gunnison Canyon the trend would continue. Meanwhile, the workload on Gary and Blake had been far too much. Early on, the notion of completing a speed run was out of the question. Without saying a word they all knew this and realized that completing the entire Moose River from beginning to end was going to suffice. They were going to take their time and scout all significant rapids or rapids Class IV and above.

Gary could sense from the behavior of the water that things were going to get even more intense. It was clear that they had reached the canyon as the river became significantly narrow. Upon entering the canyon they encountered a six mile section of continuous rapids called the Screaming Demons. They were all on high alert as they engaged relentless hydraulics. Gary knew that they would have to deal with these hydraulics for the rest of the trip through the canyon. With this in mind, he ordered Nathan to put his camera away and help with Blake on maintaining equilibrium of the boat.

At times, their boat appeared like a pinball bouncing off boulders, shifting position and angles without warning. One violent collision with a boulder caused one of the dry bags to fling overboard. It was so chaotic and hectic that the men could not risk more danger in retrieving it. At the beginning of the trip all dry bags were tied down to the boat. With the constant abuse the river was inflicting on the boat, the bag had become loose. In the boat the men often collided and crashed into each other, looking like a rugby match on a see saw. At the first checkpoint Dale witnessed their boat bouncing like a cork in the water. Up and down with violent vigor, slapping and slamming into swells the boat appeared to be out of control. Dale was nervous as he watched them careening down the river. He too knew that this was a different river than what he remembered.

After avoiding several moving whirlpools, Gary looked for an eddy to pull into for a break and to have Blake take over the rowing duties. It was a much needed break as the three men were battered and tattered. After a quick damage assessment and inventory review, they came to realize that the dry bag that went overboard contained their two-way radio. Perhaps they were too beat up and worn out to show their despair but they were all concerned about what happened. Gary was hoping to use the radio during the break to contact Dale to provide him an update. They were unaware that Dale had seen them earlier at the checkpoint. The checkpoint was high above the canyon wall with no access to the river. Even in broad daylight, they wouldn't have been able to see or hear him. Gary tried to calm his nerves but the thought of something else or someone going overboard in darkness petrified him.

They would take a much longer break than what they originally would have liked. But they needed to regroup and take some deep breaths. Plus Gary had been rowing for the last 45 minutes, over 30 minutes more than what the original plan stipulated. Everything seemed to have been altered. The river was dictating their every move. Although rattled a bit, running the entire river from beginning to end was still very much in sight.

Blake took over the rowing duties and finished moving the boat through the remainder of the Screaming Demons. After another series of chain linked rapids consisting of fast turbulent water, they finally got a reprieve from the madness. During the reprieve they let Nathan row the next four miles. It was almost as if they were stalling to get through the darkness and then get back to full speed at sunrise. Of course, with this kind of thinking it would take more than two days of rowing. However, the higher than expected speed of river current, should offset or counter that notion. Gary was wearing himself out with the myriad of reasoning and thoughts going through his mind with the darkness.

The men could only imagine how scenic and beautiful the canyon must be. They almost felt guilty passing perhaps the most amazing scenery they could ever imagine. Knowing that neither Blake nor Nathan had ever seen this section, Gary did his best in describing the intricate details of the landscape.

After cycling through several rowing rotations they found another eddy to rest their aching arms and shoulders. Nathan complained about blisters that he had on his fingers from rowing. For the first time on the trip Gary and Blake laughed, mocking Nathan's whining. They gave him a hard time on the little amount of rowing he had done. Nathan had no idea of what it was going to take to row 200 miles and the wear and tear it would have on the upper body. They were all hurting and even grabbed some muscle rubbing cream out of the first aid kit to massage their aching hands and arms.

It was clear that Gary was in charge and his knowledge of the river, especially in Gunnison Canyon, was invaluable. Even though Gary successfully ran the canyon before, it was under much safer and less floodwater conditions than its present state. Blake and Nathan had to look to Gary for evaluating the rapids ahead of them. Gary had an impeccable feel for the river and announced verbal directions to guide them on where to go in the river.

They were approaching mile 80 on the trip and were close to a quarter of the way through the canyon when they came upon the Class V; Double Z rapid. Gary wanted to scout the rapid ahead of time to understand what they needed to do. He directed Blake to move the boat into a nearby eddy. While Blake was turning the boat to enter the eddy, the speed of the current was too fast and spun the boat out. They were soon at the mercy of the river as the boat entered a swirling vortex of water. All three men became disoriented from the movement and were forced to go wherever the river sent them. Water was coming into the boat from all angles as they ran into a series of angular rolling waves. So much water had entered the boat from the waves that each of the aqua shoes the men were wearing had become totally submerged. Dry bags, food, plastic containers and other items were floating in the water inside the boat. The boat had become so weighted down from the water it took on that it produced its own waves. Once they exited the Double Z they furiously and energetically bailed as much of the water out of the boat as possible. The boat was tough enough to maneuver without water bogging it down, the enormous amounts they received from the waves was making it impossible to steer. They knew that they had to remove as much water from the boat before reaching the next rapid so that they could adequately control the boat.

Daylight was finally becoming apparent and the men felt that they had a fighting chance in navigating the rapids. The crew could now clearly see wave trains*, strainers, pourovers*, keeper holes, eddy's, drops, and boils*. The men could also clearly see the destruction caused by the extra volume of water. Many of the strainers and eddies that they came across were full of shattered tree limbs, branches and other riff raff. Slowly the cliffs rose on both sides of the boat as they dropped through a narrow slot of tumbling waterfalls into what could be described as a large bowl or gouge in the river. Gary later mentioned that the gouge was the result of a 110 foot dam that used to be there.

Soon after the tumbling waterfalls came the Lost Paddle Class V rapid. This contained one of the largest hydraulics in the canyon. Gary debated to bypass Lost Paddle and portage but felt confident they could manage it. This was going to be better than any amusement ride the men could ever imagine. Early on in the rapid both Gary and Nathan had to perform several highsiding maneuvers to keep the boat relatively stable. After going over a 10 foot drop they descended into a hydraulic. They were stuck in the hydraulic for several minutes. Finally after some strategic moves on Gary's part, they became free and were on their way again. When the boat hit the hydraulic Blake fell forward hitting his head on the bow gunwales causing a nasty gash to his nose. Gary moved the boat to safety and proceeded to apply a bandage. It was a good time to grab some nourishment and recollect themselves. As they were parked in the eddy Nathan yelled out that their cooler filled with food and drink was floating downstream. Along with the cooler was an extra oar they had for emergencies, flashlights, an extra personal floatation device and several dry bags. It was too late to retrieve the items as they were a good 100 yards downstream.

The impact with the hydraulic caused more damage than they initially believed. Watching some of their prized possessions floating downstream demolished their morale. A flood of dread had consumed them. They later discovered that the covered storage container built within the bow of the boat had been damaged allowing all of its contents to fall out. They knew it wasn't the end of the world, but it left them with a bad taste in their mouths. They knew that any contact with Dale was going to be impossible. The radio was long gone and there was no public access to the river for at least another 45 miles. This access site was a Moose River Outfitter business where they could easily restock any supplies that they would need. In the preparations for the trip Gary and Dale agreed to meet up here to check in and take care of any other needs. In fact, if the run was to be terminated or if they were unable to go further, this would be the place to pull out. Fortunately they still had trail mix and dehydrated foods stowed away in a dry bag that hadn't gone in the river. They still had their water filter to help them eliminate most of the bacteria contained in the river water.

Not long after their experience in the Lost Paddle rapid, they noticed smoldering smoke rising in the distance. They didn't notice any boats in the area and thought it was an odd place to build a fire to send out signals. They thought maybe it was backcountry hikers that had camped out. It would be rare though to see hikers in this wilderness so isolated from any organized, structured trails. Gary directed Blake to pull the boat to the river bank to check things out. Gary thought that maybe Dale had set up camp to be able to seek them out, since there hadn't been any sign of him to this point. When they arrived to where the smoke was rising no one was around. They could tell that there was a tent set up from the matted brush on the ground, but nothing else. Gary was hoping that whoever camped there wasn't a park ranger. Gary knew if they were seen by a park ranger there would be no guess work, their trip would be over instantly.

With relatively calmer water ahead, Nathan took over the rowing duties. While entering some Class III water the men heard a helicopter flying overhead. Gary was paranoid now as he believed it to be a Canadian Park Service chopper. He thought perhaps someone had seen them early on and reported them to the rangers. After closer inspection Gary realized by the model, size and absence of Park Service design logos, that it was a civilian tour company aircraft. What they didn't know was that Dale had become fearful that something bad happened to them in the upper canyon sections. After the initial checkpoint he hadn't heard any transmissions from them via radio. Gary and Dale understood how inaccessible the river was after the initial checkpoint area and based on that, Gary made it clear that he would use the radio to contact Dale. With the radio lost to the river, Gary had no way to contact him.

Dale became nervous and was unsure if he should contact the rangers. Dale was amazed that the park rangers hadn't sniffed them out as of yet. There is no doubt that if the rangers knew about this stunt they would have ended their trip long before this.

Dale found out later that the Canadian Park Service had recently laid off numerous employees and were reshuffling Yukon Rangers to higher demand regions such as British Columbia and Alberta Provinces. The rangers that were being reshuffled to Gunnison Canyon were going through orientation training as well as attending work seminars.

He didn't want to jeopardize their trip and decided to seek out a good friend that owed him a favor. Tom Grange was the sole proprietor of Yukon Wilderness Tour Company. Dale had known him for many years guiding rafts, survival training, and even sold him some drift boats. Ironically, Tom also knew Gary back in the day working in the commercial river guide business. Knowing that most of Tom's business revolved around helicopter tours, flying over the canyon was going to be his best bet to locate the crew and ensure their safety. After Dale explained to Tom the situation and who they were looking for, they quickly fired up the aircraft.

Tom wasn't surprised to hear that they were searching for Gary Moyer. After all, it was Tom that aided and abetted Gary on his legendary trip in the canyon 10 years ago. Gary had deceived the Park Service by using Tom as a decoy. Tom and another guide entered the canyon to give them the impression that they were going to run the canyon. While Park Rangers were being distracted by Tom's reckless behavior; Gary zoomed on by becoming only the third person to run the canyon successfully.

After they exchanged waves to the drift boat crew and saw that they were alright, Tom gave Dale some extra flight time scouting the river downstream. Dale wanted a firsthand look at what the crew was going to be facing. Dale was first envious of their amazing courage to do this, but horrified what he saw down below. Even Tom suggested that they must be crazy. Both of them never saw hydraulics and whirlpools this massive. "There must be 20 foot whirlpools down there", Tom said. Dale cringed when they flew over the Slaughterhouse Rapid, the largest and worst in the canyon. Under normal conditions it's considered a Class V rapid, but in its current state it's a Class VI*. They both commented that the waves in the Slaughterhouse reminded them of 20 foot breakers out in the ocean. The waves were changing and crashing in all directions.

They both agreed that it was a death trap and would rely on Gary's good judgment not to run it. Dale was confident in Gary's knowledge of the rapid. Gary certainly knew by now that the present conditions of the river would compel them to portage around the Slaughterhouse. Dale would be alarmed if he knew that they had yet to portage. Based on what he'd seen thus far he was certain that they must have portaged around Lost Paddle and the Double Z rapids.

Dale understood that it wasn't in the cards for Gary to portage. He just wasn't wired like that. He was balls to the walls and went after everything at full speed. One of Gary's philosophies and other canyon boatmen purists; if there isn't a total blockage (dam) in the river than there will be no need to portage. Dale still felt an obligation to warn Gary and the crew about the river ahead of them but it was too late. By now they were rowing in the narrowest part of the canyon. In fact, this particular section has no riverbanks. It is nothing but canyon walls with a river running in between.

Dale felt that perhaps he was overreacting and letting his emotions take over. Knowing how stubborn Gary could be, there would be no way of stopping him. Once his mind is set on something it is usually etched in stone. With the canyon walls being so close together it would be impossible for the helicopter to fly in. It would still be at least another 30 miles before the crew and Dale meet up at the Moose River Outfitters downstream.

Acknowledging increased speed in the current and turbulent water ahead, Gary ordered Nathan to stop rowing and move to the stern. Blake went to the rowing position while Gary repositioned to the bow to scout the upcoming rapid. He knew it was too early to be facing Slaughterhouse but the sound of the water was deafening much like a potential class VI rapid. Both excitement and panic began pulsating through his body. Perhaps the upcoming water was all bark and no bite. Either way the three prepared for battle as they strategically positioned themselves.

They entered the Iron Ring rapid at break neck speed slamming into large waves laced with massive boulders, over-pours and floating logs. Gary had Blake row the boat to the right to avoid large strainers occupying the middle of the river. Blake rowed too far to the right and Slam! They literally bounced off of the canyon wall causing muscular skeletal adjustments in all three men. They continued slamming into the canyon walls sometimes careening into the right side wall then into the left side wall. After several minutes of constant pounding and zigzagging they appeared much like a punch drunk boxer. At times looking up to the sky was like looking into a crevasse in the ground. The width of the river looked at times wider than the upper opening of the canyon. They prayed that nothing would go wrong because there would be no chance of rescue. If they were to capsize or fall out it would be a long, hard cold swim. Gary made it clear before the trip that if anyone gets separated from the boat in high speed turbulent water, to always go downstream feet first. This of course was common knowledge to any canyon boatmen but Gary repeated it often to Nathan.

They continued on with a warrior spirit and exhilaration as they conquered the middle canyon sections to include Rock-N-Roll, Straight Jacket, Devils Curve and Tumble Home rapids. They were knocking them off one by one building confidence at each and every problem spot.

Nathan was in his glory obtaining great video footage of the trip. If he wasn't assisting in highsiding or calling out obstructions from the bow, he mainly resided in the stern videotaping as much of the action as possible. Whenever they had a break or situated in an eddy, he would gather information on rapids (name, class, description, strategy etc.), and thoughts and ideas of what they were feeling. He wanted to expose as much of the human element and spirit as possible, revealing to the audience what is going on in the minds and hearts of these river boatmen was Nathan's mission. The more personal and intimate the better. It is these features that attract audiences and sustain their interest. Although they were just over half way through the trip he felt that he had enough material for a good 45 minute program.

Turbulent water could be heard up ahead and Gary was confident that this was the first sign that they were getting close to the Slaughterhouse. He instructed Blake to position the boat behind a large strainer. It was like listening to a fired up football coach trying to motivate and inspire his players for the big game. He assured them that once they got through this rapid it would be smooth sailing to the end. The pep talk continued with Gary suggesting to Nathan that this is what will put his documentary over the top. "After the public observes us successfully running this rapid, they will be talking about us long after we leave this world." Blake was taken aback by Gary's intensity. He had known Gary for over four years and had been in stressful situations before, but never had he seen him so excited and worked up over anything. Gary was frothing at the mouth on explaining what an event such as this would do to their legacy.

There was no doubt in any of their minds that the Slaughterhouse trumped any other whitewater rapid they had ever seen or been in. Last time Gary ran the Slaughterhouse, he was able to row the boat onto a sandbar got out and thoroughly scouted the rapid. With the water being so high he was not going to be able to do this. However, he did see a large boulder near the first bend in the rapid that he could possibly gain access to. Once on top of the boulder he could assess the rapid and come up with the safest and most effective way of running it. Although there wasn't much left for food and supplies he told Nathan and Blake to ensure what was left to be tied down.

He positioned himself in the rowing position while Blake went to the bow. Gary had become very reliant on Blake's ability in reading rivers and communicating obstacles and river features to him. Gary explained to the crew that the speed, timing and angle of their approach were going to be critical. Nathan found safe storage for his video camera and equipment, knowing that he would not need it for awhile.

Nathan had later reflected in his documentary that at this point in the trip he was feeling a lot of uneasiness in his stomach. He was unsure if it was nervous energy, excitement or both. It was the feeling of no return that perhaps was causing the overwhelming nervousness. After some final words of wisdom and inspiration from Gary, they all took a deep breath. They were off and running to destiny.

Their next objective was to get to the boulder so that they could obtain a better assessment of the rapid. As they approached the boulder, the current hijacked their drift boat and propelled them far to the right side canyon wall. It was going to be impossible to utilize the boulder for scouting purposes. They would have to try another location to get a better glimpse of what was downstream. By now the river had become enraged chaos as they were being thrown about the boat forcing them out of position. They were doing everything in their power to maintain the boat upright. It was going to be too late for scouting anything as they were now fully engulfed within the jaws of the Slaughterhouse. They were going to have to rely on knowledge, instincts, reflexes, power, quick reactions, anticipation and perseverance to get them through this monstrous whitewater. The laws of physics were up close and in person with the three men. The massive flow of water through tight canyon walls equates to huge whitewater.

There would be no turning back now as they were being rocketed through the canyon via an angry river. Gary had never seen whitewater like this before. Near the middle part of Slaughterhouse, the whitewater was so violent that it forced the bow of the boat up into the air almost like the space shuttle positioned on the launch pad. The boat had become close to vertical when Blake lost control of his grip on the gunwales and fell towards the stern.

The next series of events all happened in a blur as Nathan would later report in his documentary. On the way down, Blake had made solid contact with Gary causing him to let go of the oars. After contact with Gary, his body continued to propel downward slamming him into the stern of the boat, knocking him unconscious. Nathan later thought that it was a miracle that they were all still in the boat and that he didn't get smashed into by Blake. It just seemed that Blake was making contact with everything during the fall.

They had no way of telling if Blake was alive or not as they were scrambling to keep the boat afloat and upright. They would have to get to safety as soon as possible so that they could check his vitals and perform CPR if necessary. Gary asked if there was any sign of life or movement from Blake and Nathan said "no, nothing". Gary struggled to grab hold of the oar handles and to regain control of the boat. Gary pleaded with the river gods to show mercy and to help them find a safe eddy or location to help their friend.

The river was relentless as it continued to slam, twist, and lift the boat in all unpredictable directions. At times, Nathan got onto the boat deck where Blake was positioned and laid on top of him to keep him from being thrown out of the boat. It was an urgent situation and terror could easily be seen in the eyes of both Gary and Nathan. They desperately sought out an eddy or safe location to pull into. Despair was raising its ugly head as they did not see any relief in sight. There was nothing but whirlpools, keeper holes, sweepers, strainers and massive waves ahead of them.

At this point they would be ecstatic if they never paddled or rowed a boat again. They definitely wanted out of the boat they were in now. What they saw ahead of them was the tail end of Slaughterhouse and to conquer it Gary knew they had to keep the boat relatively straight and balanced. But in order to keep the boat balanced they would need to execute a series of highsiding techniques. Without Blake and with one person, Nathan, doing it was going to be difficult to perform. Gary knew that with the conditions they were facing, they needed the weight of two grown adults to perform this. If they could just get through the next few series of rough water they would be close to exiting the canyon and meeting up with Dale not long after that.

17

High Drama on the Moose

They handled the first whirlpool fine. Upon exiting the second whirlpool, they became sideways, eventually ramming broadside into a massive boulder. The impact was devastating as the boat flipped over dumping all of its contents into the river. Nathan was unsure what had all transpired. Other than that he heard a loud Bam! And that he was now swimming in 40 degree water. The cold water shock consumed his entire body causing him to hyperventilate. He couldn't catch his breath as he was dog paddling in a river well known for its arctic ice laden headwaters. The panic was uncontrollable as he scrambled to find Gary and Blake. If there was any doubt as to the fate of Blake being alive or dead it was pretty certain now.

Nathan frantically scrambled to find a safe position in the river so that he could locate Gary and Blake. On his initial scan of the river there was no sign of either one. The current eventually pushed him downstream to a large strainer located on the outer part of the rapid. The strainer seemed to be collecting everything in the rivers path. The drift boat was upside down moving towards Nathan and the strainer. Debris from the boat was scattered everywhere in the river. The boat had picked up momentum smashing through the strainer narrowly missing Nathan. The strainer was now broken up and Nathan was going wherever the current wanted to take him. He continued to scan for Gary and Blake but still nothing but him, the boat ahead of him, and more whitewater.

At this point the canyon had opened up and he noticed forest land and several sand bars down the river. The boat was now a battering ram propelling downstream slamming into boulders, limbs, etc. His adrenaline was at a fever pitch as he concentrated on staying alive and catching up to the boat. The boat was his lifeline as he was still deep into the wilderness. He remembered what Gary had said about keeping your feet ahead of you as you traveled downstream. His legs and back were taking serious punishment but it was better that than head first and risking damage to the brain.

The pressure to find a safe location was building by the minute as darkness had begun creeping in. He was gaining ground on the boat thanks to large sweepers*; that were slowing the boats progress. The current now was rapid but much slower than in the Slaughterhouse.

The river had also become wider and more shallow allowing Nathan to use his feet to move through the water. He finally caught up to the boat grabbing the rope that was attached to the stern. The wrestling match had ensued as he struggled to pull the boat onto a nearby sandbar. The water logged boat was near impossible to move through the water. As he struggled with the boat he slipped and fell causing him to pass the sandbar that he was hoping to land on.

The boat was now calling the shots as its momentum was now pulling Nathan along. During a quick visual inspection of the boat, Nathan noticed a good sized gash on the starboard (right) side where it had made contact with the boulder.

While continuing to float downstream, he came across several dry bags; that had fallen out of the boat. He gathered the bags with one hand and held onto the rope that was tied to the boat with the other. He noticed another sandbar ahead that was located on the left side or inner part of an upcoming bend in the river. The task would be difficult because the river current was taking everything to the right. He would have to fight the current with all the energy he had left to gain access to the sandbar. There was a series of low hanging tree limbs located on the left side riverbank. He made sure to move over to the left side long before the bend in the river where the right side current was fast and turbulent. It felt like a lifetime for Nathan to ferry* himself and the boat from one side of the river to the other. Holding onto the dry bag straps became difficult so he thrust the bags under the gunwale of the boat to keep them contained.

At this point, the boat's gunwales were well underwater allowing a tight sealed canopy or compartment. As his hand released the bags under the boat, he felt what seemed to be the bottom or sole of a shoe. He was startled and his body shuttered with terror. Nathan quickly moved his hand back from under the boat to continue on toward the sandbar. At least now he had one hand free to help pull the boat or to anchor onto something.

Once he made it close to the riverbank, he began using the tree limbs as an anchor one by one to control his progress. He remembered Gary often saying whatever you do, do not grab an overhanging limb or object while in the boat. It was never explained to him what not to do if you weren't in the boat. He was running out of ideas and felt that this was his only feasible option. The shallow riverbed had made it possible for Nathan to stabilize his footing and he eventually pulled the boat onto the sandbar.

18

Survival Mode

Initially he was relieved on safely reaching the sandbar, but his mind was racing all over the place. He still had no idea what had happened to Gary and Blake or where they ended up. What was it that he felt under the boat? He knew that he had to work fast as darkness had fully embraced the region. He no longer had his headlamp and doubted that there was any left in the boat or dry bags.

While attempting to move the boat upright, he became terrified on finding out what he had touched earlier. He tried to compose himself as he finally got the boat upright onto its hull. He immediately saw the two red dry bags that he placed in the boat earlier but what he saw next took the air out of him. It was Gary! The instant shock turned to dread and anguish. Nathan felt as if someone had punched him in the gut as he observed Gary's lifeless body. There was no safety helmet on Gary's head and it was nowhere to be found. Gary's life preserver was still firmly in position on his neck and shoulders, but his legs were mangled and contorted.

When Nathan turned the boat onto its hull, Gary's body was still physically attached to the boat. One of Gary's legs was entrapped under the crossbench he was sitting on to row. The other leg was tangled up in rope that was attached to the stern. He rushed to get him released from the boat by untangling the rope from one leg and moving the other leg out and away from the crossbench. The leg trapped under the crossbench appeared to be so drastically distorted that Nathan knew it had to be broken.

The dry suit pants that Gary was wearing were ripped everywhere. With so much darkness upon him, he was seeing only outlines of images and was uncertain of what he was seeing. The only glimmer of light available was what was transmitting from the full moon above. Gary was not responding to any of Nathan's questions to him adding even more misery to the situation.

As Nathan kneeled next to Gary to get a closer look and to perform CPR, he noticed that his eyes were open. He didn't know what to think of this and was scared and overwhelmed with his limited knowledge of medical emergencies. The only training he ever had in CPR and first aid was through the military. He never had to use it before, and felt hopeless and frustrated that he wasn't more competent in performing what he needed to do to help Gary.

While checking for obstructions in Gary's nose and throat he noticed that his cheeks felt warm to the touch. Nathan was somewhat confident from watching movies and various forensic programs that warm skin was more of a positive sign than cool skin was.

He got closer to Gary to see any signs of breathing. Nathan became elated as he could distinguish Gary's chest rising and falling. It was a faint rise and fall but Gary was breathing and Nathan saw hope. Nathan shook Gary to see if he could get any reaction but the only movement was coming from the rise and fall of his chest.

He then placed his fingers on Gary's wrist, and couldn't find a pulse but when he checked his own, he couldn't locate that either. Nathan put his ear to Gary's chest and heard the heart beating. Something in his memory bank was telling him to time Gary's pulse to see if it was normal. He remembered that 72 beats per minute was considered to be a normal heart rate.

When he went to time the pulse he noticed that his digital watch was not displaying anything on the LCD screen. The watch had become water logged, or damaged most likely, from all the collisions with the many objects in the river. Either way he was going to have to manually estimate the rate on his own. He became flustered and couldn't focus on the heart beat and counting seconds at the same time. Multi-tasking was something he was never good at. His best guess was 32 beats per half minute.

Nathan was perplexed on Gary's situation. Something in the way Gary looked made the condition appear like more than just being knocked out or unconscious. He was hoping that Gary was knocked out and that in a short time he would come to. Nathan tried to be positive especially with the fact that Gary was breathing evenly – short breaths, but consistent – and his heart was beating regularly.

Nathan would keep him warm and make him as comfortable as possible. It was urgent that Nathan immobilize Gary's mangled leg. He went into the nearby woods to find a tree branch or limb and some vines to wrap the limb to the leg. It was to be a crude treatment but necessary. Something had to be done to Gary's leg to prevent further damage. He had to rely on his hands and moonlight to find something that would help keep the leg straight.

After applying the makeshift splint to Gary's leg, he pulled the boat onto higher ground on the sandbar. The last thing he needed was the water level in the river rising high enough to wash them and the boat downstream. To ease his mind and to secure the boat to the shore, he grabbed the rope from the dry bag and tied it to the closest tree he could find. He flipped the boat over onto its gunwales and dragged Gary under it to provide shelter and a little warmth.

Once he got the boat and Gary in a safe position, he went to inspect the dry bags to see if he could find anything useful. He knew that they would need a fire to warm their cold, water drenched bodies. Nathan was shivering as he rifled through the bags hoping to find a flint or some sort of fire starter. Between the two bags he found dehydrated fruit, rope, towel, iodine tablets for water, hand bailer, duct tape, knife and his camera. It was going to be a long hard cold night without a fire.

Nathan grabbed the towel and dried Gary off the best he could. After laying the towel over him he went searching for a rock or stone to help make fire. By now Nathan was delirious and found it difficult to put one foot in front of the other. He had been deprived of sleep for almost two full days. Even if it was broad daylight he wouldn't have been able to see straight. Never in his life had he felt so weak and dehydrated. The only nutrition he had was some trail mix about 18 hours ago. If it wasn't for the river water that he had been gulping since falling in, his body would have been seized up by now. However, the side effects from ingestion of untreated river water had been taking its toll. He was having major stomach aches and cramps. Ever since landing on the sandbar he had been plagued with constant nausea and diarrhea. It was only impulse power and the commitment to Gary's wellbeing that he was even functioning at this point.

His search for finding rocks for a flint became an arduous task as all he could muster up was smooth round stones. These stones most likely had been rounded and smoothed from many years of constant pounding from the wind and violent thrashing of river water. He gathered some fine dry pine twigs nearby to help with the initial lighting of the fire. After grabbing the knife he saw in the dry bag, he began striking the blade of the knife with the rock.

No sparks were to be seen and exasperation had taken over. There was not going to be a fire tonight.

Nathan hated the thought of drinking more river water but he knew that he had the iodine tablets to treat it with. He retrieved the hand bailer from the dry bag and scooped it into the river to collect water. Once the water was securely in place he dropped two iodine tablets into it. After the tablets dissolved he then tried to pour some light drops into Gary's mouth. He tried to pay attention to any swallowing movements but observed nothing. However, the small drops of water seemed to be going down his throat. Nathan rechecked Gary's vitals to ensure that he still had a pulse and was still breathing. As he laid his head down onto Gary's chest to confirm his breathing and heartbeat, he collapsed, eventually rolling off of Gary and onto his side.

After getting up the next morning, Nathan lifted the boat up and away from where Gary had been lying to position it back on its hull. Upon lifting the boat upright, he became distressed when he noticed that blood was splattered near the back end of the boat. He began to tremble on what he would find next. Would there be a body part or something else disturbing that he'd find in the boat. He was not able to see the blood the night before because of darkness. Now he could see everything. His mind was jumping back and forth on the source of the blood. The blood may be the sign or reason why Gary was currently unconscious. Could it have been from Blake as a result of his violent impact with the boat after his fall? He even checked his own body to see if he was bleeding. He found cuts, contusions, scratches, bruises and dried blood up and down both legs as well as his hands and arms. All of this was compliments of the many sharp boulders and tree limbs from the Moose River.

He quickly went to Gary to inspect his head and body for lacerations and any signs of blood. There was no sign of blood or cuts other than where his dry suit pants had been ripped. The blood coming from the pants appeared to be from superficial cuts and nothing deep. He did, however, feel several large bumps located on both the front and back side of the head.

While inspecting for blood, he reassessed Gary's vitals to ensure his heart and lungs were still functioning. There had been no change in his breathing and heartbeat since last night. His mind continued to race about Gary's condition. He remembered watching some medical program that featured patients who had been in a coma for months or even years. Then they would suddenly snap out of it and wonder how long they'd been asleep. Nathan continued to talk to Gary praying that he would eventually respond. Gary was unconscious and it appeared to be a coma. It was almost like Gary was asleep, except he couldn't wake up. Everything appeared to be working except he couldn't eat or drink.

While leaning over Gary to check his heartbeat, he was overwhelmed with the smell of human feces. It was clear that Gary's other bodily functions were working as well. There had been many firsts for Nathan on this trip and cleaning someone else's waste was going to be yet another one. At the same time, he was going to clean the wounds on Gary's legs as well as reapply a stronger splint to his broken leg. After carefully removing the splint and pants, he did everything he could to fight back the nausea. He held his breath while using nearby leaves and grass to clean him. Nathan washed him down with treated river water that he had already prepared earlier.

For the splint, he found a stronger, straighter piece of wood to use and snugly attached it with duct tape. Nathan cleaned what was left of Gary's pants and placed them back onto his legs.

After he thoroughly washed and scrubbed himself down he finished eating what was left of their food – six pieces of dried apricots. He could no longer fight off the hunger pains that had been persistent for well over a day and a half. He felt a sense of guilt and selfishness while chewing the fruit. What if Gary came out of his coma and there was no food for him? Nathan felt shame knowing that if Gary came to he would need the nourishment much more than himself.

Nathan was almost certain that Dale was expecting them over twelve hours ago. He was in a quandary whether they should stay put and build a fire to emit a smoke signal, or repair the boat and head downstream where it would be assured they could get help. From his vantage point, the river appeared to be fast with much less whitewater. If anything, the river seemed to be calmer than what the last mile or two was coming into the sandbar. They were well beyond the canyon and the surrounding landscape had opened up creating a much wider river basin.

Nathan had the sense that they were getting close to the outfitter company that Gary mentioned as their meet-up spot with Dale. With their river maps long gone from the Lost Paddle rapid, there was no way of knowing their specific location or distance to upcoming landmarks. Time was of the essence and Gary needed medical attention as soon as possible. There was no telling how long it would be before the authorities would find them.

He felt an overwhelming urge to fix the boat and get to someone that was medically qualified to assist Gary. In addition, he had no confidence in starting a fire to produce a smoke signal. Last night he only found smooth round stones that couldn't produce a spark when making contact with the knife. He searched again to see if he could find a rock or stone that would make a good flint. After finding nothing that would work, he reaffirmed to himself that the best option would be to move downstream and find help.

In order to get back out on the river, he was going to have to repair the gash on the boat. He filled the hole with whatever he could find and patched it up with five or six layers of duct tape both on the inside and outside of the boat. While patching the boat, he couldn't help but marvel at the versatility and strength of duct tape. He remembered his father using it for everything and anything. Nathan wished he had a phone to call his dad to let him know that he was using duct tape to patch a hole on a boat. To inform his father that perhaps duct tape was potentially going to determine the outcome of a real life or death event. He thought that if the duct tape helped the boat enough to get them to safety, he would be more than happy to provide a testimonial or become a spokesperson for the product. He continued to reflect on his family and on life in general. Perhaps he was creating a defense mechanism to escape the reality of what had transpired and what may evolve in the next few hours or even days. More specifically, he wanted to shield himself from the reality of what had happened to Blake and from what was going on with Gary.

Before loading Gary onto the boat he attempted to give him some water. With the hand bailer half full of water, he slowly poured drops into Gary's mouth. Gary's gag reflex activated instantly as he coughed, spit and sprayed water in Nathan's face. He continued to choke prompting Nathan to move Gary's head over to the side. He then placed his face downward with his left hand and pounded on his back with his right. Not sure what he was doing Nathan became frantic and was concerned that he may have made Gary's condition worse. He was disgusted with himself, knowing that before Gary was unable to drink so why would he be able to now. Eventually the coughing stopped and the water cleared from Gary's mouth and throat. Nathan had to accept the fact that Gary was not going to be able to eat or drink. He kept telling himself not to force the issue.

Nathan had no idea what a panic attack was but he felt that he might be on the verge of one. There was no ignoring the fact that he was trembling and experiencing heart palpitations. The anxiety he was feeling was intense and something that he had never experienced before. Everything seemed to be collapsing in on him. At one point he yelled out, "I need help! I can't do this alone! Please help me!"

He paced back and forth hoping to regain his composure. It was critical that he stay strong for both Gary and himself. Besides his compromised mental state, his physical state was weak and severely deprived of much needed nutrition. The six pieces of dried apricots he had the day before did not touch his raging hunger. Before getting out onto the river he needed to find something with protein to help sustain him.

Catching fish in the river became a debacle as his homemade spear proved to be inadequate and ineffective. He was fortunate to find some worms near the riverbank that he quickly devoured. This was not the time to be a discerning eater as he was open to just about everything. Even the river grass was fair game. Several snails and caterpillars became part of the eating frenzy. Never in his wildest dreams could he ever imagine eating snails, worms and caterpillars. He was just hoping not to get sick from them.

Nathan pulled the boat out into the river to ensure that his patch job with duct tape would suffice.

There was some moisture build-up on the tape located on the inside patchwork but nothing significant. He pulled the boat back up onto the sandbar to load up Gary and the dry bags. It was a mighty task getting Gary up and into the boat. With his right hand he tilted one side of the boat (closest to Gary) downward to the ground while pulling Gary onto the boat with his left hand. The process was time consuming and physically taxing on Nathan's body. Once he safely positioned Gary onto the boat's deck, it was time to move on.

They ended up departing the sandbar much later than what Nathan had originally planned. It was already late in the afternoon and time was becoming more critical than ever. It felt strange for Nathan to be back out on the river rowing and now captain of the boat. He felt anxious and vulnerable without a river map. He was praying that the river would not present any more surprises or dangerous situations.

19

Search and Rescue

Early in the evening on the previous day, Dale had been overcome with worry and reported the crew and boat to the park service. He reported them missing and was concerned for their well being. Dale informed rangers that he was supposed to meet up with them at the Moose River Outfitter Company somewhere between noon and 5:00 PM. There was no sign of them as of 7:30PM and he felt that something had gone wrong. Dale urged the rangers to employ rescue operations to search for the three men. Rangers explained to Dale that there would not be any rescue attempt due to high winds and darkness. They ensured Dale that they would initiate search parties at first light on the next day.

Dale was enraged and animated at what he perceived from the rangers as a lack of compassion. After being consoled by another ranger, he regained his composure and continued conversing with them on search and rescue strategies.

The next morning, Dale was upset to find out that the park service rescue helicopter was grounded due to maintenance issues. Dale called his friend Tom Grange who had helped him out before to see if he could use his services once more. Tom's wife, who was also the secretary of the business, answered the phone and explained to Dale that Tom would be out all day running a survival training exercise in the Yukon River Gorge. Dale was at the mercy of the park service to find the crew. Dale's never ending persistence allowed him to become an active participant in the search and rescue operation. The park service deployed all available personnel to scour the river. Resources involved in the search included; solo and tandem kayaks, dories, backcountry rangers, local outfitters, Canadian Mounted Police and motorized boats and rafts. It was a multi – disciplined effort.

20

Perseverance

Up to this point Nathan had kept the drift boat moving steadily as they mainly encountered class II and III water. At times he felt like he had zoned out and was fully entrenched on his rowing technique. He had learned quite a bit from Gary and Blake on manipulating the boat in whitewater and he was using it to his full advantage. With all that had happened he felt as if he temporarily was at peace with himself. It was the feeling of quiet inner peace that he had not experienced in a long while. Rowing the boat was creating a powerful distraction from the true reality that was taking place. However, nothing in the world was going to distract the reality of what Nathan saw next.

He became sick to his stomach yet again. It was the last thing he wanted to see – a surprise! Up ahead was a fork in the river. Without the river maps he was screwed and had no idea which way to go. The current in both sides was relatively the same and there were no distinguishing characteristics to assist him on where to go. Nathan was hoping to see signs that would guide him in the right direction. He was looking to see which side had the higher amount of water volume, depth, width, speed, drop-offs, whirlpools, strainers etc. There was nothing for him to go on. It was going to be a flip of the coin.

There was no way to tell if the division or fork in the river was a bypass of some sort or if the other branch was another separate river. He couldn't even rely on an educational guess. He was too inexperienced to even have an educational guess. All the speculation and guessing that he struggled with had turned his innards into an erupting volcano. He was confident that even without a map Gary and Blake would know exactly where to go. Although Gary was in a coma, Nathan asked him out loud, "which way should we go?" Of course there was no answer and Nathan was left to decide on his own.

Early in the run and long before the crew reached the Gunnison Canyon, he noticed several forks in the river. For each fork that they encountered they stayed to the right. Perhaps it wasn't logical or maybe juvenile but he decided to bear to the right. It was an uneasy feeling but he resolved to stick with his gut feeling. The landscape remained consistent with what he had observed before entering into the fork. By all accounts he believed it to be the same old Moose River he had been married to for the last three days.

On two occasions they came across sections of the river that had been totally blocked off from fallen tree limbs. He was unsure on how recent the trees had fallen. They could have fallen as recent as that morning for all he knew. It felt odd to him that this particular section of river would have this type of an obstruction.

It seemed to him that there should have been more boat or raft traffic through this particular area. It appeared to be a safe, fun part of the river, for play boating. If there was a good amount of boat traffic through here you certainly wouldn't have to deal with all this congestion. Nathan found it hard to believe that reputable rafting outfits in the region and the park service would neglect this section of the river. All he knew was that these obstructions were stopping their momentum moving downstream and killing their time. At each portage he had to exit the boat, grab the rope attached to the bow and pull it out onto the riverbank to bypass the blockage. It was a backbreaking and time consuming endeavor.

With the late start and the two major portages to contend with, he decided to look for a camping area to spend the night. Executing the last portage drained all the energy he had left. He also wanted to take advantage of the remaining few hours of daylight to help him look for food and to start a fire.

A fire was going to be critical for them as they needed warmth throughout the night. Nathan's body had been breaking down rapidly and another night of bitterly cold temperatures in the Yukon wilderness would be devastating. They desperately needed a fire to repel the mosquitoes that had caused them havoc the night before. Equally important was the fact that they needed to establish a fire to provide a signal to get the attention of rescue personnel.

It was a mystery to him that there had been no sign of rescue aircraft or watercraft. Besides wildlife, they hadn't seen a living sole since observing a fisherman on the riverbank on day one of the trip. They had been missing for over 36 hours from their scheduled meet – up time with Dale. Nathan thought for sure somebody would have been searching for them long before now. The possibility of them traveling on the wrong river loomed large to him. It was possible that the reason they haven't seen any rescue personnel was because they were not on the Moose River. If there were any rescue operations taking place, it would be taking place on the Moose River. He kept beating himself up internally over the possibility that he may have made the worst decision of his life. Perhaps if they had stayed to the left of the fork they would have been in safe hands by now and Gary would be receiving the proper care that he so desperately needed. Hindsight was killing him as he continued to dwell on what he should or shouldn't have done back at the divided river.

Nathan rowed the boat into a small but safe inlet located on the right side of the river. Before arriving at the inlet he noticed several apple trees and various berry bushes located above the riverbank. The riverbank alongside the inlet was relatively flat and open making it a good location for smoke from a fire to be easily seen from afar.

After pulling the boat out of the inlet and onto the bank he secured the boat by tying the bow rope to a nearby tree. He went into the forest to find leaves and pine boughs* to use for their bedding. Once the bedding was in place he carefully pulled Gary out of the boat and onto the pine boughs. As he was pulling him he noticed that his broken leg appeared to have enlarged and had become visibly swollen. Nathan had found that the leg was infected and he was worried about gangrene* setting in. He began to cry and wondered out loud how much more could they take? While standing with his arms high in the air and looking up to the sky – he screamed, "Please help! Enough already!"

Once he had Gary in a safe position, he then gathered some large limbs and vines to build a makeshift lean-to* against the boat. It was crude and primitive at best but it would provide a much needed form of shelter. He simply leaned the limbs and branches onto the side gunwales of the boat, and placed large leaves, pine boughs or anything that would provide adequate cover. He then relocated some of the original bedding items such as the leaves, pine boughs into the lean-to. Once completed he carefully repositioned Gary by slowly dragging him into the lean-to and onto the bedding.

With darkness fast approaching he went searching for rocks that could be used as a flint. Like before, all he could find was smooth round stones. Finally after an hour he discovered some black rocks that were chipped and layered. He quickly pulled out his knife to scrape the rock to see if there was any spark. After five or six scrapes on the sharp edge of the rock with the blade of his knife, he had a spark. For the first time in a long time he smiled. He came back to Gary with a smile on his face saying, "We will be warm tonight." He realized that he was a long way from success and knew that he would need tinder* to catch the spark.

Along the riverbank he found some birch bark and dried grass. He began shredding the dry birch bark with his knife until it looked like hair. To keep the fire going throughout the night, he gathered small pine and birch twigs, branches and larger pieces of wood. To help create a visible smoke signal he collected large green leaves and other green plants and vegetation. Nathan had seen a wilderness themed reality television program that illustrated several strategies to utilize in drawing attention or signaling for help. Throwing green vegetation over a fire was one of the strategies that they described.

It was clear that Nathan didn't want to run out of firewood in the night because he had gathered enough wood to build a small city. Once he found a safe and suitable place near the lean-to for building a fire, he began the process of igniting it. The process was long and tedious, but he eventually got the fire started. He sensed a feeling of accomplishment and elation for the fact that they would be warm tonight and that they wouldn't have to fight off the mosquitoes.

Seeing the fire he created ignited a surge of adrenaline and positive energy. With the exception of a Y Indian Guides summer camp, he had never had to perform such a lofty task. The camp experience was all about learning and having fun; this was wildlife survival in its most primitive form. Whatever shortcomings he felt in dealing with Gary's medical condition or the decisions he'd made out on the river, making the fire more than compensated for all of that.

While the fire was going he ventured up above the riverbank to investigate the berry bushes and apple trees that he saw earlier. It was a smorgasbord of fruit that he could only have dreamed of. He went crazy picking blackberries, raspberries and apples. It didn't matter if they had holes, worms or even rotten to the core. He couldn't stuff them in his mouth fast enough.

Nathan wanted to create as much smoke from the fire as possible. So anything in the wood pile that resembled the color green he threw onto the fire. He threw so much green vegetation onto the fire that it almost went out.

He continued to produce smoke up until sunset. Still there was no aircraft, no boats, and no people – nothing. It was the same old sights and sounds. This night however, they had fire and that was something to be grateful for.

His earlier assumption of someone searching for them was correct. Little did he know, the morning after Dale made his missing report to the park service, there had been a full scale search and rescue mission in effect.

It was difficult to fall asleep as he continued to reflect on all that had happened. He could not clear his mind about Blake and where he ended up. Gary's vitals had seemed to improve as Nathan assessed Gary's heart rate at 71 beats per minute and his pulse felt stronger and steady.

Before going to sleep he gathered more wood to pile onto the fire, hoping that it would be enough to sustain the fire throughout the night. While entering the lean-to for the night he heard the sound of a wolf. At first he was startled with the sound but realized there was nothing he could do about it. He was confident that the fire would more than likely keep the wolf away.

Before Nathan was up and moving for the new day, search and rescue teams were in full motion. The helicopter that was incapacitated for maintenance issues two days earlier was getting ready for takeoff. Three motorized rafts and dory boats were getting into position to scout the river for the three men. Canadian Mounted Police had their own patrols scouring the Moose River. Even some of the local rafting companies, to include Blake and Gary's outfit, volunteered some of their own watercraft and personnel to the cause.

Nathan started the morning off by producing another series of smoke signals hoping that someone was in the area. Before heading out onto the river, Nathan noticed that his crude duct tape patchwork on the boat was all but destroyed. He tore out what was left of it and replaced it with fresh duct tape.

It was another laborious task loading Gary onto the boat. Adding to the difficulty was the fact that it was raining heavily, making it next to impossible to establish a solid grip on anything. While he was loading Gary onto the boat he couldn't help but gawk at Gary's poor mangled leg. It was an awful site to look at and the urgency to find help was a life and death situation. He quickly moved the boat back out into the inlet, jumped in and began rowing. The rain had subsided clearing the way for breathtaking scenery. But his beautiful surroundings were the last thing on his mind. He was only focused on one thing and that was to find help.

After rowing for about 10 miles or so he noticed that the river current had become much slower. The depth of the river had become shallow causing the boat to bottom out on numerous occasions. Each time they bottomed out was cause for frustration as he would have to exit the boat. Once out of the boat he would have to pull on the rope to get it through the shallow water. It was at this point that he seriously considered rowing back upstream to the fork. Once at the fork he would then take the left side hoping that help would not be far away. He knew that in order to row against the flow of the river (upstream) would be a monumental task. It was a chore that he was not in any physical condition to undertake. He would stay the course and deal with the shallow water and sporadic bottoming out.

Dale had been assisting in the search with a park service motorized raft crew when he heard a transmission come in on their two-way radio. A body had been found trapped underneath a strainer in the Class III* rapid called Whiplash. The dead body was found by a local kayaker that had volunteered in the search. The ranger who received the message looked at Dale and said we may have one of the men. Dale's worst fears had come alive and now he was going to have to help authorities provide a positive identification of the body. Dale couldn't come to grips with what was happening and what this would do to either Jennifer or Chelsea.

After traveling approximately 20 miles downstream, they arrived at a boat access site where the body was being prepared to be transported to the Whitehorse County Coroners facility. Dale was visibly shaken as the Canadian Mountie uncovered the body bag. Dale was horrified at what he saw. He confirmed to the Mountie that it was Blake Henson. Once he made the identification, he then had to fill out paperwork pertaining to his knowledge of Blake and any details that could assist authorities regarding the accident.

He resented the fact that he had to reiterate everything on paper that he had already previously reported in his initial missing persons report. Time was everything and he insisted to get back out onto the river to help find Gary and Nathan.

Nathan's frustration from rowing in the shallow water became even more pronounced as it felt like the boat was being sucked downward. At this point he was yearning to see some whitewater again because he knew that whitewater would certainly get them down the river faster. The blisters on his hands had all busted open from having to row harder in the shallow water. The fluid from the blisters had become like epoxy sticking to his hands on each stroke. His mind was wandering so much he had no idea where they were or how far they had come. He felt like he was a zombie or robot, constantly looking forward seeing only the front of the boat, Gary and the river ahead. The same routine over and over again; row breathe, row breathe, row, breathe.

21

Salvation

Something that didn't seem routine for a change was the sight of a roof top tucked away in the trees. It was straight ahead and about a mile away. Could it be possible that he was hallucinating? After all he hadn't seen a man made structure in over three days. Then he heard a dog barking. Nathan couldn't believe what he was hearing and seeing. Up ahead was a wooden platform that appeared to be a boat dock with a dog barking on it. Almost as if the dog was waiting for its master to come home.

As he rowed the boat to the end of the dock, Nathan heard loud yells of "Rusty, hush up"! A large bearded man came trotting downhill to see what the commotion was. As soon as the man came into his sight Nathan began shouting "help us please, please, can you help us!" Nathan looked up to the man with tears in his eyes and pleaded again to help them. The man grabbed the rope attached to the bow and tied it to the dock. After helping the man into the boat they lifted Gary and placed him onto the dock. Then they picked Gary up, placing his left arm over Nathan's right shoulder and his right arm over the man's left shoulder. The trip up the hill seemed forever as Nathan struggled to support Gary's weight on his pain riddled right shoulder. As they were walking up the hill, the man told Nathan that it would take at least 30 minutes before any first responders would arrive.

They would have no choice but to drive Gary to the hospital themselves. Nathan asked the man if he had a phone that he could use to call the Canadian authorities about a missing person. The man informed Nathan that there was no cell phone coverage and that they had no landline phone. He added that him and the misses were old school and very traditional. "When we come out here it's all about us and mother nature." "We leave all comforts at our home in Carmacks," the man said.

After loading Gary into the man's pick-up truck, they rushed to the hospital. The man grabbed Nathan's hand to shake while introducing himself as Walter Graylock. During the drive to the hospital Nathan asked Walter what the name of the river was that he lived on. It was clear that Nathan was having a hard time focusing and thus was not an active listener. Walter reminded Nathan that he didn't live there, and that it was only a summer cottage. Walter explained to Nathan that he and his wife lived in Carmacks, farther north. He added that they usually spend time there in June, July and August. "The river you came in on is the Elk River." Nathan's heart sank and he began to cry inside. It was heartbreaking to hear this.

He agonized over the amount of energy and precious time that was expended and lost because of his wrong decision to go right instead of left. Walter continued to explain that the Elk River branches off of the Moose and is often called the Junior Moose. Because of damming and lack of recreational demand, it has progressively wasted away. It once was a thriving river with a lot of activity. There used to be several commercial rafting companies and outfitters that utilized the river. That's all gone now. Walter mentioned to Nathan that it is extremely rare to see anybody paddle through there. "If we do see someone, it's usually by mistake." Nathan quickly quipped with "don't tell me, because they went to the right instead of going to the left?" Walter confirmed with a definitive, "You got it!"

They arrived to the hospital where Nathan alerted a nearby emergency room nurse that they needed help. Hospital staff members whisked Gary away on a gurney leaving Nathan alone to wait and pray. In the meantime, he thanked Walter for saving them from their misery and asked for his address and phone number. People will want to know who found us and who brought us back to the world.

While waiting for news about Gary, Nathan used a hospital phone to call the Canadian Mounted Police regarding Blake and to inform them of his situation. The phone conversation with the Mounties quickly became somber as he was informed about Blake being found in the river. He knew that this kind of information was going to be a strong reality but he nevertheless took it hard. He was told that they had already contacted Blake's family. They told Nathan that after final processing of the body by the coroner, Blake would then be sent back to Montana for burial. The Mounties then advised Nathan to remain at the hospital so that they could get information from him and to file an incident report.

Dale was still with a rescue squad deep in the Yukon wilderness unable to receive a signal on his cell phone. Nathan felt pressure and an obligation to call Gary's wife, but he didn't have her phone number. Both his phone and Gary's phone that had all her information was at Dale's home.

After six hours of waiting, he finally received an update from the doctor. At first the doctor was reluctant to give patient information to a non family member, but they realized that this was a special circumstance. Nathan felt frozen in time as the doctor explained to him what seemed to be a never ending list of problems pertaining to Gary's condition. The doctor must have felt like he was talking to a mannequin as everything he was saying to Nathan seemed to bounce off of his emotionless gaze. However, when Nathan heard the words gangrene and amputation in the same sentence, he quickly snapped out of his trance. Shortly after Gary broke his leg, infection infiltrated the leg causing a major loss of blood flow. The lack of blood flow caused the tissue in the leg to die allowing gangrene to set in. There were no other options so the leg had to be removed. The coma was considered to be low grade and the prognosis was good. The doctor felt that Gary should come out of the coma in less than a week and should fully recover within six months.

By this time, Dale had learned about Nathan's call to the Canadian Mounted Police providing to them information on their whereabouts. Once Dale arrived at the hospital, Nathan updated him on Gary's medical condition.

Later on, Dale had noticed that Jennifer had called him several times leaving voice messages. After finding out from Chelsea what had happened to Blake she went into a panic wondering about the status of Gary. She wanted to talk to Dale and nobody else – not the Mounties – not the park service, just Dale. She knew that if she received a call from the Canadian authorities it would crush her. She saw what it did to Chelsea and there was no way she could handle that.

Dale called Jennifer to explain all the details. It was difficult to hear Jennifer crying on the other end. She would leave the children with friends and catch the next plane out to be with Gary.

It was tough on Chelsea not having Jennifer by her side but she insisted that Jennifer go to Gary to be with him in his time of need.

22

Conclusion

Back in Montana, the funeral for Blake was highly emotional and gut-wrenching. Nathan had established a strong bond with Blake over the last couple of months and felt compelled to attend the funeral. He wanted to meet Chelsea and to offer his personal condolences to her. He was always impressed and envious of Blake's admiration and love for her. Many times he saw Blake beam with pride and joy over her and the reality of him becoming a father.

Most of Blake's personal effects traveled with him to Montana, however; there were a few items that had been overlooked. One such item was a 14kt gold locket that contained a picture of Chelsea and Blake together in the mountains. It was their favorite picture of them together. As Nathan presented it to her, she fell to her knees crying. It was a picture that they both cherished. After consoling her, he then gave her a DVD containing outtakes and interviews of Blake during the Yukon 1000. Also on the DVD was video footage of Blake paddling on the Yukon River and whitewater rafting on the Moose River.

When Nathan arrived back home in Seattle, there was a notice in his mailbox requesting him to pick – up and sign for a package that was at the post office. After returning home from the post office he noticed the name Dale Quinn on the parcel. He grabbed a knife, opened the box and inside were two red dry bags, his camera, towel and water tablets and a note that said, "Thought you could use this, Dale". Nathan couldn't believe what he was looking at. Items that will forever be linked to the wildest and scariest ride he had ever been on. A ride filled with sorrow, elation and despair. The ride included the full range of emotions. The items in the box may need to go in some archive or personal museum he thought. Ever since opening the box, flashbacks of his river run was coming fast and furious.

In his line of work, video cameras are his livelihood, his temple, his everything. But this particular camera somehow got left behind, lost in the mayhem and chaos. At the time Walter met him at the boat dock with his dog barking and Gary wasting away in the boat, the last thing on his mind was to grab the camera.

Is it possible that after everything that had happened, Nathan vanished into a realm of not knowing why he participated in such a suicide mission in the first place? The events surrounding Blake and Gary made it possible for Nathan to become oblivious to his intended mission for joining the crew.

But now the contents inside the camera may be the recipe to help everyone move on. He was amazed at how the camera had been relatively unscathed by the never ending onslaught of water, limbs and boulders. The dry bags that contained the camera had certainly lived up to its intended purpose as everything looked to be intact. After replacing the camera's batteries he reviewed each of the memory cards to ensure that they were alright.

Nathan resolved to the fact that yes, there will be initial kickback on making the documentary, however the greater good will prevail by helping individuals such as himself, Gary, Dale, Jennifer and yes, even Chelsea go to the next step. The documentary could be the final therapeutic tool to assist people in finding closure with all that had happened.

After struggling for so long to move past the death of Blake, she soon transitioned into the miracle of life as Chelsea gave birth to a healthy baby boy. Both Chelsea and Blake agreed that they were not going to name the baby until after its birth. But Chelsea knew long before this that if the baby was going to be a boy, she would name him after his dad. It was a surreal experience for Chelsea to move from one end of life's spectrum to the opposite end.

After eight months of painstaking editing, rewrites, audio revisions, narration redo's etc., Nathan was finished with the 45 minute documentary. With the approximately 15 minutes of commercials, public service announcements and station identification and promotions, the program should comfortably fit inside a one hour time slot. As promised to Gary, Nathan would ensure that Gary have the final say and approval on everything before releasing the final product to the public.

At this point Gary had fully recovered from the coma and had been successfully fitted for a prosthetic leg. Nathan called Jennifer and Gary to inform them that he had completed the documentary and was hoping to fly to Bozeman, Montana to meet with them on getting their feedback.

Jennifer expressed her concerns over the whole idea and believed that Chelsea would have to be on board as well. Nathan was fine with that, even suggesting that the four of them review the documentary with each person providing their own evaluation on it. Once all revisions addressing their concerns were made he would have them review for one final time before releasing to the media outlets. It was important for Nathan to release the film with everybody comfortable and onboard. It had to be unanimous.

After several months of additions, omissions and various tweaking it was time for the final review. Nathan had invited all of them to his Seattle production studios to do a private showing of the film.

Nathan had creatively and masterfully presented the most compelling masterpiece, vividly illustrating the trials and tribulations of their journey down the Moose and Elk Rivers. At first there was silence, but near the end waterworks began to flow and whimpers and sniffs could be heard. It was a piece of work that Blake would have been proud and honored to be a part of. The final scenes highlighted on Blake's down to earth style and loving life personality. It was a powerful finish to such a wonderful film. The film ended with a picture of Blake that was provided by Chelsea showing his electric smile and alluring facial features. On the screen below the picture of Blake were the words, "This film is dedicated to Blake Henson, a man who loved life and lived it to the fullest."

During the film, Jennifer helped hold Blake Jr. to give Chelsea a break. While scenes of Blake were being shown, she looked at Blake Jr. and pointed to the screen and said, "That's your daddy". Without hesitation Blake Jr. said the words 'dada'. Hearing this, Chelsea broke down and became inconsolable. It was heart wrenching watching her trying to regain her composure. As Chelsea grabbed a tissue to wipe her tears she told Jennifer that the words 'dada' were the first words he had spoken.

The production that Nathan created was a success and it was well received by everybody.

After getting back home from Seattle, Gary decided to visit Blake's grave site. He hadn't been to visit yet and had mixed feelings on why. Perhaps a visit to the grave would trigger all the feelings of guilt that he had for getting Blake involved in paddling. He still thought that there was underlying tension between him and Chelsea. He felt that she had displayed subtle animosity toward him for his endless desire to pursue the thrill of adventure. Gary believed that she may have thought that he coerced and persuaded Blake to do these extreme stunts. The fact is, Gary only got the ball rolling and Blake took it and ran with it.

While at the grave site he paused to say a little prayer. He placed a maple wood paddle that he made in his shop at home. It was a paddle similar to what Blake used in the Big Sky Regatta and the Yukon 1000 river races. On the blade of the paddle Gary engraved Blake's name and the words, "To the best partner a river boatman could ever have. Rest in Peace Blake".

*Glossary of Terms

Bailer – device or mechanism that assists in the removal of water from the boat.

Boil – unpredictable currents pushing (boiling) to the surface, usually caused by rocks.

Confluence – junction of two rivers or forks of a river.

Drop offs – short, well-defined rapid or section of a rapid.

Eddy – area of calm water behind or downstream of an obstruction, where the water flows against the current.

Ferry – a maneuver used to move back and forth across a river.

Gangrene – a potentially life threatening condition that arises when a considerable mass of body tissue dies. It may occur after an injury or infection.

Highside – jumping to the 'high' side of the raft to level it out and prevent capsizing when it's pinned against a rock or stuck in a hydraulic.

Hole – a swirling vortex of water where the river flows over an obstacle and drops toward the river bottom instead of continuing its downstream flow, leaving a pocket into which upstream current flows.

Hydraulic – is formed when water falls over a ledge, rock, log, or other object. When the water falls of the object, it picks up speed and when it hits the water below, it rolls.

Keeper – a dangerous hole that can hold a swimmer or boat for an extended period of time.

Lean – to – rough shelter whose roof has only one slope. Protective covering that provides protection from the weather.

Pine boughs – a pine tree branch, especially a large or main branch.

Portage – is the practice of carrying watercraft or cargo over land, either around an obstacle in a river or between two bodies of water.

Pourovers – rocks with flat tops that are just under the surface of the water.

Put-in – the place where the whitewater trip begins.

Scout – locating a strategic position in the river to inspect a rapid.

Strainer – an obstacle, such as a tree, that lets water flow through freely but traps swimmers, boats, and debris.

Sweepers – trees fallen in or heavily leaning over the river, still rooted on the shore and not fully submerged. Its trunk and branches may form an obstruction in the river like strainers.

Take-out – the place where the trip ends.

Tinder – combustible material used to ignite fires by basic methods. Anything that begins to glow under a shower of sparks.

Wave Train – series of standing waves or a runout of a rapid.

Classification of Rapids:

Class I – moving water with a few riffles and small waves, few or no obstructions.

Class II – easy rapids with smaller waves, clear channels that are obvious without scouting. Some maneuvering might be required.

Class III – rapids with high, irregular waves. And narrow passages that often require precise maneuvering.

Class IV – long, difficult rapids with constricted passages that often require complex maneuvering in turbulent water. The course may be hard to determine and scouting is often necessary.

Class V – extremely difficult, long and very violent rapids with highly congested routes. They should be scouted from the shore. Rescue conditions are difficult, and there is a significant hazard to life in the event of a mishap. The upper limit of what is possible in a commercial raft.

Class VI – the difficulties of Class V carried to the extreme. They are nearly impossible and very dangerous. Class VI rapids are for teams of experts only. They involve risk of life. Class VI rapids are not commercially raftable.

About The Author

Derek Miller is originally from Encinitas, CA. He currently lives in Salisbury, NC with his wife Kathleen, and daughter Brittany. His son, Derek is currently living in Tacoma, Washington.

Derek loves to read, write, travel, hike, kayak, swim, climb, and anything else that involves the outdoors. He is a free lance journalist for a local newspaper. His free lance writing consists of climbing, hiking, canoe/kayak adventures, and travel documentaries. He has written the short stories: The Majestic Emerald Isle, Quest for the 50 Highpoints, Land of the Morning Sun, The Ascent of Mt. Whitney, Worlds Longest Single Day Flat Water Canoe Race, The Last Frontier, Craters of the Moon, Mesa Verde, Historical Capital of Bohemia, Not Any Ordinary Rock, Journey to the World's Tallest Volcano, The Big Ditch, & Ancient Ephesus; which can be found as e-books on Amazon.com. He is currently writing other documentaries, short stories, newspaper articles, and a non-fiction novel.

Derek is a Licensed Massage Therapist with credentials in Aromatherapy, Reflexology, Lymphatic Drainage, Neuromuscular and Swedish massage.

He is also a registered Gemologist for The Jewelry Cove; which can be seen at www.thejewelrycove.com.

Printed in the USA
CPSIA information can be obtained
at www.ICGtesting.com
LVHW092324081224
798652LV00006B/170